The Sack

'Dad said, "I'm redundant. They've made me redundant." And his voice sounded funny. He sounded frightened and sad and angry all at the same time. His dad sounded frightened.'

When Shane's dad loses his job, everything changes, slowly at first and then faster and faster. But although Shane and his family have to give up so much that is familiar, Shane finds that, in their new life, they still have what is most important.

By the same author

The Sack

Christobel Mattingley

Illustrated by Simon Kneebone

Puffin Books

Puffin Books
Penguin Books Australia Ltd
487 Maroondah Highway, PO Box 257
Ringwood, Victoria 3134, Australia
Penguin Books Ltd
Harmondsworth, Middlesex, England
Viking Penguin, A Division of Penguin Books USA Inc.
375 Hudson Street, New York, New York 10014, USA
Penguin Books Canada Limited
10 Alcorn Avenue, Toronto, Ontario, Canada M4V 3B2
Penguin Books (N.Z.) Ltd
182-190 Wairau Road, Auckland 10, New Zealand

First published by Penguin Books Australia, 1993
1 3 5 7 9 10 8 6 4 2
Copyright © Christobel Mattingley, 1993
Illustrations Copyright © Simon Kneebone, 1993

Typeset in 13½/15 pt Goudy Old Style by Midland Typesetters, Maryborough, Vic.
Made and printed in Australia by Australian Print Group, Maryborough, Vic.

National Library of Australia
Cataloguing-in-Publication data:
Mattingley, Christobel, 1931- .
The sack.

ISBN 0 14 036558 3.

I. Title.

A823.3

For Martin and Chris
who believed in me and for me

I was born in 1931 in the middle of the Great Depression. My father, an engineer, was out of work and had contracted tuberculosis, a much dreaded disease at that time. My mother used to buy six pennyworth of scrag mutton and a bunch of soup vegetables each Friday to make soups and stew. But the family really survived on a weekly basket of food Grandmother sent from the country. My first teeth dropped out when I was very young and I was 'gummy' until I was almost eight. My mother, now ninety, still recalls those days.

In February 1992 I was in the supermarket one day. Our church collects groceries for needy families. It was the week before school was to go back and I was looking for items which mothers would like to put in school lunch boxes for their children. I woke up in the middle of that night and found *The Sack* had started writing itself in my head.

Contents

• One •
Redundant

Shane still remembers the day his dad lost his job. There was so much he didn't understand. So much he had to learn. And the learning was lonely, though lots of people tried to help.

Dad came home early that day. Shane was surprised but his mum didn't seem to be. She didn't say, 'What a nice surprise!' or 'Why are you home so early?' She just stared, her dark eyes somehow growing bigger and darker.

Dad said, 'I'm redundant. They've made me redundant.' And his voice was funny. Then he said another word. He sounded frightened and sad and angry all at the same time. His dad sounded frightened.

Redundant was the word that made his dad sound frightened. It made Shane think of the big lumbering elephant at the circus. It sounded slow and clumsy. And somehow Dad looked slow and clumsy, which he really wasn't. He looked old and he looked awkward when he put his arms around Mum.

Redundant. The elephant at the zoo always looked sad. Standing in the same spot, marking time with its big solid feet, swaying slowly, staring at the bars and palm trees painted on the concrete walls. Walking round the same track, past the same things, day after day, year after year.

Redundant. Shane had seen an angry elephant in the wild tearing and trampling, crushing everything in its path as it trumpeted its rage. It had scared him, even on TV.

The other word wasn't a good word. Shane knew from the way his father said it. It seemed to taste bitter on his tongue. But Mum didn't say, 'Not in front of the children, Mike.' She just hitched Shelley-baby onto her left hip and put her right arm round him. She snuggled her head on his shoulder and for a moment they both seemed to forget Shane was there.

Then his father pulled away. 'I'm going to the pub.'

'Mike, no!' Mum pleaded. 'I'll make a cup of tea.'

But Dad was halfway out the door. She ran after him. 'Please don't go. Think of the children.' But it seemed his father was suddenly deaf. She pulled at his arm and he shook her off. He was like a stranger. 'At least give me the money before you go,' she begged, hanging onto the door handle.

He wrenched it from her grip, with another ugly-sounding word. Mum stumbled and fell against the door frame. Shelley squalled. Shane ran to his mum. But his father did not turn back. He flung himself into the car, revving it furiously, so that as he backed down the drive a blue burst of acrid smoke belched from the exhaust.

Shane held Shelley and looked at his mum. Her face had gone pale but her eyes were like black holes and there was a big red mark across her cheek and forehead. 'I'll make you a cup of tea, Mum,' he offered. 'Nice and strong.' He was surprised at the sound of his own voice. It was funny too.

Then she surprised him. 'No,' she said. 'Not strong. Just one spoon in the pot. That'll be enough.'

He heard Tom and Jed calling from next door. But he didn't go out. He made the tea just as his mum had said and carried it to her. It looked unusually pale in the mug, pale as her face. He sat down beside her on the sofa. 'Shall I read to you, Mum?'

She nodded. She liked to hear his reading and he usually brought home a book from the school library to read with her. Even Shelley enjoyed it. But today his mother didn't seem to hear. It was as if she had suddenly gone deaf. Like his father. When Shane stumbled over words, she didn't notice, and when he got stuck she didn't help.

He was disappointed. It was a new book with funny pictures. 'Look, Mum,' he said, as he turned each page. But she didn't even smile. He showed Shelley the pictures, telling her about them until she fell asleep.

Tom and Jed knocked at the door.

'Go out and play now,' his mother said. She didn't say 'Thank you for reading' or 'It's a lovely book'.

Shane went out.

'Your dad got the sack too?' Jed asked.

'No,' Shane replied. 'He's redundant.'

Tall Tom and stringy Jed punched each other,

laughing loudly. 'That means he's got the sack,' Tom said and they both looked pityingly at Shane. He felt stupid because he had not known what the long lumbering word meant.

The sack. The sack. And he thought of Father Christmas and presents.

'Bet your dad will come home roaring drunk,' they said.

'Bet he won't,' Shane declared.

But in the night he was startled awake by a crash of bricks and a crunch of metal. A car door slammed, his father swore loudly, then was ringing the bell. 'Open up, Jen. I can't find my key.'

Shane heard his mother run to the door. 'Not so loud, Mike. You'll disturb the neighbours.'

'Stuff the neighbours,' his father shouted. 'Let me in.'

Shane heard the lock click and the screen door open. 'Do be quiet, Mike. You'll wake the children.'

His father roared. His mother screamed. There was a thud and a sound of shattering. Shane guessed it was the vase on the table near the door. Grandma's vase. He pulled the doona over his head. But he could still hear his father shouting above the television. Then when the shouting stopped there was the sound of sobbing.

In the morning Grandma's vase had disappeared. 'Don't walk on the carpet in your bare feet,' his mother said. 'I broke a glass last night on the tiles by the front door and it went into smithereens. There could still be some slivers I missed. They flew everywhere.'

Shane knew she was really talking about Grandma's vase. Cut crystal it was, with a starry pattern that caught the light when the sun shone through the window, making rainbow patches on the wall and dancing figures on the ceiling. Mum had called it 'the fairies' house' when she was little. She had thought the golden glimmers were fairies. Shelley might have thought that too, if the vase could have been there when she was growing up.

He went outside, trying not to think about it. It felt as if the slivers of glass were inside him, sharp and shining, cutting all he knew. The car was still in the carport. And its front left mudguard was dinted and scratched. He remembered the sound in the night and looked down the drive. The left gatepost, where Bimbi always sat to welcome him home from school, was a tumbled heap of bricks.

Tom and Jed appeared above the fence. 'Told you your dad'd get drunk.'

'How did you know?'

'We got ears, we got eyes,' Jed said, jerking a thumb towards the gatepost, then towards the car.

7

'No, I mean how did you know he would get drunk?'

Tom said matter-of-factly, 'They always do.'

'Always?'

'Always when they lose their jobs, stoopid. Don't you know anything?'

Shane didn't feel like sharing the times he remembered his father drunk. Three times. Years ago after hearing that his best friend had been knocked off his motor bike and killed. Last year when he'd come home from the office party, very red in the face, talking loud in a slurry way.

His mum had said, 'You're drunk, Mike.' But he had replied, 'No, just merry.' 'What is there to be merry about?' she had asked quietly. 'I'm sh-shel-shelebrating,' he said. 'I've still got my job. Some poor guys copped it today.' His mother hadn't said any more. 'Ta ta. Bye bye. It's been nice knowing you,' his father said to nobody and didn't sound merry at all.

'Sit down while I make you some coffee,' his mother had said, and he had sat down heavily, almost squashing Bimbi. The cat had yowled and hissed, and Shane was shocked when his father kicked out. 'Stupid animal. Should never have been allowed inside.'

'But, Dad,' Shane had protested, 'you know she always sleeps in that chair.' His father hadn't answered. He'd put his head in his hands and when his mother came back with the mug, his father was asleep. Snoring. Shane had never heard him snore before.

Last night. Shouting and smashing. And this morning snoring again. Shane had heard the horrible sound when he'd gone early to the toilet.

'We ought to know,' Jed said, interrupting Shane's thoughts. 'After all our dad has lost his job three times. And he's not the only one around here.'

Shane nodded. It was easier.

Tom added, 'And if you don't know much yet, you soon will. Come on, Jed, or else we'll be late, and so will you, young Shane. You'll

have enough troubles without getting into more.'

School was ordinary. Ordinary people. Doing the usual things. Until lunchtime. When Shane opened his lunch box he was surprised. And disappointed. His mum nearly always slipped in some little treat – a chocolate biscuit, a cheese stick or a handful of sultanas or peanuts. Sometimes it was a packet of chips, or if it was hot, money for an ice block. Today it contained only sandwiches and an apple. After he'd eaten them he tried not to notice the kids who were rustling their packets and crunching their chips. But he knew then that things had changed.

• Two •
'Put it Back'

When he got home Mum was waiting with Shelley in her pusher. Shane bent down and tickled her. He loved to hear her laugh. But his mother said, 'Hurry up, Shane. Have a drink, then we'll go shopping.'

'But aren't we going tonight with Dad in the car like we always do on Thursdays?' He looked forward to the fun of going all together, Dad pushing the trolley while Mum pushed Shelley. He used to ride in it when Dad took it out to the car. Now of course he was too big for that. Now he pushed it himself if it wasn't too full. After they'd done the shopping they'd have ice-creams and look around. Dad would sometimes buy a book for him to read while he and Mum had coffee. Or they'd go to the library.

'No. Dad's not coming today,' his mother said. 'We're walking.'

'Walking?' It didn't seem far in the car, but it was a much longer walk than Shane expected.

He felt hot and bad-tempered picking his way along the footpath through heaps of clay thrown up by roadworks. 'Why are we walking?' he whined.

'To save petrol.'

'Why do we have to save petrol?'

'Because your father's been retrenched.'

Retrenched.

He looked at the trenches along the kerb. Like a continuous grave. Like the grave he had seen at his grandmother's funeral. Was being retrenched like being put in a grave? Finished? Dead? He shivered, although he was hot. It seemed as if something had already died in his mother. Mum was always so warm and smiling, ready to share a joke. But since yesterday she was like a dead light globe. Nothing came from her no matter how hard he pushed the switch.

It was a long trench. Perhaps the whole family got buried in it. Dad, Mum, Shelley . . . Shane, even Bimbi. And redundant was shovelled over the top like heavy hard lumps of clay. Retrenched. Stifling.

In the supermarket he pushed the trolley, but it had a cranky wheel and he kept bumping into Mum and Shelley. A woman got annoyed when he ran into her, and then he toppled a stack of cartons. His mother grabbed the trolley, saying sharply, 'You take the pusher. We can't afford any accidents.'

12

Shane said, 'Sorry, Mum. I didn't mean to.'

But she didn't seem to hear. It was like shopping with a stranger. She was much slower than usual making up her mind about some things, but walked straight past things they often bought, like ice-cream and lemonade. They came to breakfast cereals. Shane took a large packet of Coco Pops. 'Put them back,' his mother said, taking Cornflakes.

'But I like them best,' Shane protested.

'They're too expensive. We can't afford them,' she said.

Shane pulled a face at the Cornflakes. 'Oh, Mum,' he said, but she had moved on.

At the biscuit section Shane chose two packets, orange-cream and raspberry. 'Put them back, Shane,' she said, taking one plain assortment.

'But I don't like them,' he said sulkily.

'Then you'll just have to learn,' she replied, pushing on.

Still sulking he ran after her with a big packet of mixed creams. 'It's not fair. Can't we have these instead?'

'No. Put them back, I told you. We can't afford them.' Somehow she sounded more scared than cross.

Shane wondered. A Ford was standing red and shiny in the carport. With a crumpled mud-guard. The car Dad washed each week and polished till it looked as bright as the apples Mum put in his lunch box. Did they have to eat dull biscuits to get the car fixed? A ford was where the river crossed the road by the old gum trees, where the bamboos grew in tall rustling clumps, where Tom and Jed took him sometimes catching yabbies, building cubbies. What did mud and bamboos have to do with orange-cream biscuits that crunched and melted in your mouth? Afford meant money, he knew. Didn't they have any now?

His mother had passed the pet foods. 'Bimbi, Mum, Bimbi,' he reminded her, taking three cans.

She put one back, then stopped by the pasta and took six packets.

Shane asked, 'Are we having pasta every night this week?'

'Every night every week.'

Every night? 'Yuk!' Spaghetti was good once in a while. All slithery red with tomatoes and savoury with onions and bacon and cheese. But Mum hadn't put any bacon or cheese into the trolley. No onions or tomatoes either. Just tomato paste.

By the checkout were the little model cars he loved collecting. He picked one up. 'Put it back,' his mother said. 'You've got plenty.'

'But I haven't got this one.'

'Tough,' was all she said.

'Can't I have it?' he pleaded. But she took no notice.

'It's not fair,' he said. But nobody listened.

She paid and packed everything back into the trolley. There was a lot less than usual. But it was still too much to carry. His mother pushed the trolley across the car park and out into the street.

Shane said, 'But you can't take the trolley home. It belongs here.'

'Plenty of people do,' his mother said and pushed on. He had to hurry to keep up. Shelley-baby was grizzling and Shane felt cross and thirsty himself. 'Gee, it's hot. Can't we stop a moment in the shade?' But his mother didn't seem to hear and went on. He caught up again, whingeing, 'It's hot, Mum.'

'I heard you the first time. Do stop complaining.'

And then Shane felt hot outside but cold, chilled icy inside. Home at last, he went to get a drink. 'There's no cordial, Mum. We should have bought some.'

'We haven't got money for cordial. You can have water. Then you can take the trolley back.'

'Back?' said Shane. 'Now?'

'You were the one who didn't want to bring it home,' his mother reminded him sharply. 'Hurry up now and don't spend the dollar.'

She didn't even look at him, but bent over Shelley with a cup of water. Shane had never known her to be so snappy and distant. It was as if her smiles had all disappeared with the light fairies from the rainbow vase.

He trudged off, pushing the cranky trolley which veered and yawed so that he wanted to kick it. And although empty, it seemed to weigh a ton, the heavy word rolling inside – redundant, redundant, and the crazy wheels clattering and rattling – put it back, put it back. He felt as if everyone was staring at him and hoped his friends wouldn't see him.

At last he reached the supermarket again and shoved the crazy trolley into the rack. It locked in and the dollar clicked out. Shane grabbed it gratefully. Then he went in just to look at

16

the model car. It was small, red and shiny. It would have fitted in his pocket so easily. He'd just hold it for a moment.

The checkout girl recognised him. 'Hello,' she smiled. 'Come back to get the one you want? Your mum given in after all?'

Shane shook his head. 'I've only got a dollar. And that's for the trolley I returned. Mum said not to spent it. We can't afford it. Dad's been made redundant.' He blurted out the horrible word.

'Your dad's lost his job, has he? That's bad luck. It's hard when there's no pay packet coming home. No wonder your mum couldn't let you have the car.' She looked at him kindly. 'Now you'd better put it back and take the dollar home. She'll be waiting. It's good you returned the trolley. Some people don't. See you next week.'

Shane walked home, the coin tight in his sweaty palm. His hands still hurt from gripping Shelley's pusher and the trolley. His legs were aching and he could still hear put it back, we can't afford it, ice-cream, Coco Pops, cordial, cream biscuits, toy cars, cat food . . .

The gatepost was still a collapsed heap. The hall table was bare. No rainbows glowed on the passage wall. His father was slumped in a chair in the lounge. Shane said, 'Hi, Dad.' His father grunted. His face was yellowish with black stubble showing through and his breath smelt. 'Bad luck about the gatepost, Dad. I'll help you fix it.'

His father didn't answer. Shane waited a moment. His father didn't look up. Shane went out to the kitchen slowly.

His mother was trying to feed Shelley, who was turning her head and pushing the spoon away. 'Here's the dollar, Mum.' He put it on the bench with a satisfying clink. He waited for a word or a smile. But there was none. His mother just kept shoving the spoon at Shelley-baby. It seemed as if she was still deaf. And dumb. And numb.

He picked up Bimbi and went outside. She was warm and soft and pleased to see him. She began to purr as he rubbed his hot sore hands through her fur. They sat together on the back step. 'We'll fix the gatepost, Bimbi. At least we can make it tidy.' He fetched a broom and bucket.

Bimbi sat watching as he began picking up bricks and stacking them against the fence. Tom and Jed appeared. Jed picked up two bricks still stuck together. Tom picked up Bimbi.

'Give us a hand, Tom,' Jed said.

'I'm minding Bimbi,' Tom replied.

'She doesn't need minding,' Shane said. But Tom took no notice.

'You walk to the supermarket?' Jed asked.

Shane nodded.

'*And* took the trolley back?' Jed sounded incredulous.

'I suppose your mum wanted the dollar,' Tom stated.

Shane nodded.

Jed got the last bricks stowed neatly inside the fence. Shane swept up the crumbled lumps of mortar.

'Phew,' Jed sighed. 'I'm hot. Can we come in for a drink of cordial?'

Shane shook his head. 'There isn't any.'

'Don't be dumb, Jed,' Tom said over Bimbi's head. 'They can't afford cordial now. How are they gonna pay the mortgage?'

'Nah,' said Jed. ''Course not. No chips either, or ice-cream, or Coke. Come on, we'd better go.'

Tom put Bimbi down reluctantly and they disappeared.

Mortgage. Mortgagee. Walking from the supermarket Shane had noticed signs on several houses saying 'Mortgagee sale'. What did that mean?

• Three •
Porridge!

Next morning when Shane came to breakfast his
father was already at the table with the newspaper spread out. But he wasn't reading the front
part, which he always did before he went to
work, or even the sports pages. He was reading
the back, the long narrow tight columns without
pictures.

'Hi, Dad.'

His father had shaved and was wearing an
office shirt and tie. Shane was puzzled. 'You going
to work after all, Dad?'

'I hope so, Shane. I'm going looking for some,
anyway.'

'You'll find it, Dad. For sure.' Shane couldn't
imagine anyone not wanting his dad to work for
them.

Mum smiled. 'That's what I said too, Shane.'
Suddenly it seemed as if the rainbow was glowing
on the wall again and the light fairies were
dancing. Shane kissed his mum as he took his

21

lunch, and hugged his dad. 'Good luck.'

Lunch was disappointingly dull again. His mouth watered when he saw classmates with lime ice blocks. But he couldn't bring himself to ask for a suck, even from his best friend.

Dad came home soon after Shane and brought Mum a bunch of flowers. Her eyes lit up as she took them. 'You got a job?'

He shook his head. 'It's to say I'm sorry. For the other night.' She hugged him and Shane could see tears in his eyes. He wished they'd hug him too. But they didn't seem to think of it. His mother put the flowers in a honey jar on the hall table.

Dad spent all Saturday and Sunday reading the back of the paper, marking parts, phoning and writing letters. There was no chance for Shane to play computer games. The printer chattered and whirred as sheet after sheet rolled out. 'My CV,' his father said. 'People want to know what you've done.'

'CV?' Shane said. CV, TV, mortgagee. Redundant, put it back, the sack . . .

'Curriculum vitae. It's Latin for details of your life.'

'Is redundant Latin too?'

'I guess it comes from Latin, though I hadn't thought about it.'

'What's Latin?'

'It's an old language used two thousand years ago by a very important nation, the Romans.'

Shane remembered Roman soldiers had crucified Jesus. Knowing it was Latin wasn't making it any better to think about, he decided. He watched his father addressing envelopes and inserting the carefully folded letters and CVs.

'I'll seal them and stick on stamps,' he offered.

'Good bloke,' Dad said. 'Then we'll walk along and post them. They'll be delivered tomorrow. I might start getting answers by Wednesday or Thursday.'

Shane looked at the pile of letters. The postman would be busy.

In the street some nature strips were dead and in some gardens shrubs were dying and lawns needed cutting. On the fence of one house was a mortgagee sale sign. Shane wanted to ask his father what it meant, but he had turned away and the look on his face made Shane hesitate.

On Monday when his father came home, he asked, 'Any phone calls or messages?' But his mother shook her head.

On Tuesday it was 'Any phone calls or letters?' And again his mother shook her head. Wednesday was the same. So was Thursday.

It seemed the postman hadn't been busy at all.

Shane and his mother walked again to the supermarket with Shelley-baby. This time Mum surprised him by choosing different brands. 'But we don't usually have that sort,' Shane exclaimed as she took a bottle of sauce with a plain label. 'We always have the parrot.'

'We can't eat the parrot,' his mother said.

They came to breakfast cereals. Shane's hand hovered longingly over Coco Pops. Then he moved to Cornflakes. But she had already taken a packet of rolled oats. 'Put them back. We're having porridge.'

'Porridge! Porridge? But I hate porridge!'

'What's wrong with porridge?' But obviously she didn't want to hear, because she moved on, saying, 'Dad grew up on porridge.'

'That doesn't mean I have to like it,' Shane muttered. But she wasn't listening and Shelley didn't care.

Everything his mother chose had a plain label. It was hard to recognise some things and he had to read the words. 'Are we having things without pictures because they're cheaper?'

She nodded.

'Because Dad's got the sack?'

She nodded again. 'No vitamins in pictures.'

Shane looked at the shelves of enticing labels. 'When will Dad get a job again?'

His mother stopped, staring at her list. 'God knows.' She began pushing towards the checkout.

Shelley lunged at a colourful packet. 'Put it

back, Shelley,' Shane said firmly. He took it from her and put it back. She began to howl. 'You can't have it, Shelley. I'll show you pretty pictures later.'

At home he helped unpack and carry everything inside. Then he turned the trolley round and without waiting to be told started pushing it back. The checkout girl recognised him. 'I wish all our customers were as honest as you.'

On the way home he passed a church where the noticeboard said: HURTING? GOD CARES. COME INSIDE AND TELL HIM. He paused. It looked rather big and strange. He walked slowly along the path, up the steps into the porch. The door was open as he went in. For a moment he thought there must be lots of vases like Grandma's, because there were lovely rainbow patterns on the walls. Then he realised it was the sunlight through the coloured windows.

He sat down to look. A kind-faced woman came from a side door. 'Hello,' she said. 'Isn't it pretty?' She sat down beside him. Shane was glad there was someone to enjoy it with. It didn't seem to matter that they didn't talk. Her not talking was different from Mum and Dad's. That had made him very uncomfortable, raw inside, cold and aching, tired of waiting, waiting for a smile, a hug, a word. With this lady the silence was like a warm blanket, cosy and comforting. He felt happier than he'd been for days.

'Can I do anything for you or your family?'

'Mum said, "God knows." About Dad's job.'

'He does too. And He cares. You can be sure of that. But He mightn't be saying anything yet.'

Shane felt disappointed. Just like Mum and Dad. 'Well, I'd better be getting home then. I returned the trolley, see.' He showed her the dollar. 'Mum'll worry if I'm too long.'

'Come with me just one minute.' She led the way through the side door, into a room with a big cupboard which she opened. It was full of groceries. 'Is there something your mum couldn't afford today?'

'Coco Pops,' Shane blurted out.

'Oh, I don't think we've got any. But would you like chocolate biscuits?'

Shane nodded and she put a packet in his hand. Her smile made him feel as if the rainbow was inside him. He ran home and burst into the kitchen to show his mother.

'Where did you get them? You didn't spend the dollar? No, of course not,' she answered herself. 'They cost more than that.'

'A lady at the church gave them to me. Have one, Mum. Now.'

They sat side by side nibbling, making their biscuits last as long as possible. When they were finished to the last smear, Mum turned and smiled. She hugged him. 'Sorry, Shane. I've been

27

a bit down in the dumps and grumpy since Dad . . . ' she stopped, unable to go on.

'Got redundant,' Shane finished for her. 'I know.'

'You see, it means we won't have much money until he gets another job. That might take time. So we have to be careful.'

'Mum, I understand.' He felt much better now she was talking to him. Talking to him like a grown-up. Not treating him like a baby, or as if he wasn't there. He knew she was hurting inside too, but at least she had smiled. 'I'll take Shelley outside to play, so that you can get on with the cooking.'

After tea they gave Dad a chocolate biscuit with his coffee. He looked at it suspiciously. 'Where did this come from? You didn't go spending money on chocolate biscuits, did you, Jen?' he said accusingly.

She shook her head. 'No. Shane was given a packet by a lady at the church.'

'Charity,' he said sounding as if he had a bitter taste in his mouth. He pushed it away. 'Keep them for Shane's lunch.'

Next day Shane found a chocolate biscuit in his box. It was the first treat since his dad had become redundant. 'What's charity?' he said to his teacher.

'Why do you ask?'

'A lady at church gave me a packet of these

yesterday. And Dad wouldn't have one. He said they were charity.'

'That's the best sort of biscuit you could have,' Miss Williams said, 'because charity means love.'

Shane took a bite. It tasted sweet and satisfying, melting over his tongue. 'Is that a Latin word?'

'Yes,' she said. 'It comes from Latin.'

'Like redundant.'

'Yes. If there are any other words you wonder about, just ask. We could make a list.'

Shane thought of mortgagee. He wondered how a mortgagee biscuit would taste. They would be the dull ones in a mixed assortment. Somehow he thought his father would like them even less. He decided not to ask about mortgagee and enjoy the biscuit, to the last licking of fingers.

• Four •
Recycle

On Friday the flowers in the jar were dead and there was a letter in a long white envelope on the hall table. His father seized it eagerly, but screwed it up and threw it away without a word after reading it. His mother put a cup of tea in his hand and he sat at the table without drinking. She was clanging saucepans and came back quickly with plates.

'Dinner's early tonight. I thought you'd be hungry after such a long day.'

Shane couldn't see it had been longer than any other day.

But his father understood. He smiled. 'It's okay, Jen. I won't go to the pub every knock-back. I know we can't afford it.'

Shane noticed tears in his mother's eyes. He wondered why she wasn't smiling.

On Saturday after mowing the lawns, Dad said, 'I'm selling the mower.'

His mother said, 'Mike! What about the

lawns? We don't want the place getting run-down, in case we have to . . . ' She stopped when she saw Shane, who was playing with Shelley in the next room.

'Have to what?' he asked, but nobody answered.

His father said, 'I've thought of that. Dad's got the old hand mower in his shed. Shane and I'll go and get it.'

His mother said, 'We can't afford an ad in the paper.'

'I've thought of that too. I'll put notices up at the newsagent and supermarket.'

Shane thought they would go by car. But they travelled by bus. Right into the city, where he

rarely went, then on another bus in another direction. It seemed much further and took much, much longer. It was good sitting beside Dad instead of behind, having his whole attention, discussing what they were passing – shops, signs, statues, parks, factories – things he hadn't seen before. Dad knew where to get off and they walked from the bus stop to Grandpa's.

Shane had never much liked the house. It had a funny smell and was dark, with blinds drawn so the furniture would not fade. But he loved Grandpa. GP with his wrinkled brown face, his eyes like shining blue pools under the cliffs of his white brows, his big square hands with dirt in the cracked hard skin, hands that could do anything.

And it was always interesting to poke about in the shed among the stuff GP had brought from the farm. It was a big shed without glass in the window so the swallows could come and go to their nest in the rafters. It smelled too – the warm smell of oil cans, the dry smell of wheat bags, the salty smell of seaweed GP collected for his garden, the hot smell of blood and bone fertilizer and the metallic smell of old implements whose use Shane did not know.

'Look, Dad, what's this?'

But Dad, in another corner, did not hear. 'Ah!' he exclaimed. 'I knew it was here!' sounding like the dad Shane had always known, not the redundant dad.

He was holding a long handle, its bar smooth with sweat and dark with dust. 'Give us a hand, Shane.' Shane moved paint cans, an empty oil drum and a bag of lime, and his dad extricated the mower.

Shane looked at the long open cyclinder of curved blades. 'How does it work, Dad?'

'Show you in a minute. Let's find the catcher first. It'll be here somewhere. It's a triangular canvas bag on a metal frame.'

Shane looked around the walls where coils of rope, lengths of chain, old overalls and welding goggles hung on nails. He pointed. 'Is that it, Dad?'

'Sure is, Shane. Well spotted!' Dad reached up, lifting down the saggy looking contraption and giving it to Shane to carry outside while he took the mower. GP didn't have much lawn. His yard was mostly vegetable garden. But there was a patch of grass under the clothes line. Dad wheeled the mower across and showed Shane how to attach the catcher.

'Right! We're in business!' He sounded quite excited as he pushed the mower. The blades spun with a sudden clatter and the cut grass flew up in a surprised green cloud which settled in the old yellowed canvas catcher. 'What about that?' he grinned.

'Can I have a go? Let me, Dad.'

Dad handed it over. 'Your turn.'

It wasn't as easy as it looked. But Shane had just got it moving with a bit of puffing when GP came out carrying a tray with three mugs of Milo and three big biscuits, the biggest biscuits Shane had ever seen.

'That's a good old sound. Not like those noisy motor jobs,' he said. 'And you can smell the grass.'

'Environmentally friendly,' Shane's dad laughed. And GP's eyes sparkled like the sea on a summer day.

Shane sipped his Milo slowly, enjoying its chocolatey warmth in the sunshine. He felt like the yellow sunflower by the shed, tall and straight with its face to the light, as he listened to Dad joke with *his* dad.

'Keep a thing long enough . . . ' GP said. 'People say my shed's full of junk, but I say, just you wait and see.'

'Can we see some more?' Shane asked.

But his father said, 'Not today. We can't afford the time.'

And it seemed as if a cloud went over the sun. 'We can't afford the *time*?'

'Time's money today, Shane,' his father explained. 'If we catch the next bus back we can still use the same tickets. Any later and we'll have to pay again.'

'Well, you haven't got time for bush biscuits,' GP said and Dad laughed. 'But you have time to oil the mower while Shane and I pick oranges. Nice for his lunch. Juice for Shelley too. And what about some rhubarb for a pie? Remember the pies your mother used to make? Let's dig up a crown for you to take home to grow. Doesn't take much looking after.'

Shane ran to fetch a spade. He liked the thought of planting a crown. GP levered a plant out carefully. 'Not the sort of crown you could offer the Queen,' he laughed, 'but it's not called Ruby Red for nothing. You'll get a few pies out of this crown, I promise.'

'Now for oranges. They'll only take a minute.' It was true. The oranges hung on the tree like Christmas decorations. They filled a big cloth bag while Dad wiped his hands and put the oil can back. GP put in the rhubarb, tied the bag and showed Shane how to sling it.

'It's a flour bag,' Shane said.

'Yes, and you look like a swaggie,' GP laughed. 'But don't forget your bush biscuits – iron rations for the journey. You won't have time to make damper on the way home.'

He popped a packet of seeds into Shane's pocket. 'Radishes. Easy to grow and quick. Grand with bread and cheese.' He waved them a cheery goodbye.

Shane couldn't wave. It took both hands to hold the bag steady. So he called back instead. 'Thanks, GP. See ya.'

The bag was heavy and Shane was glad it wasn't far to the bus stop. He wondered what the driver was going to say about the mower and whether people would stare at them and laugh. But his dad didn't seem worried. He was whistling, just like he used to.

Five

Food for Thought

'Okay here?' Dad asked the bus driver.

'Well,' the driver demurred. 'That space is for pushers.'

'This is a pusher all right,' Dad said.

'Don't I know it!' the driver laughed. 'I'd sooner be behind the wheel of this any day. Okay there and the lad's bag too. If it's not livestock.'

'Only oranges and rhubarb,' Shane assured him. 'Mum'll make rhubarb pie tonight.'

The driver smacked his lips. 'Rhubarb pie. My mother used to make them. Wish I was on your route. I'd stop off for a serve.'

Shane grinned at the thought of the bus stopped outside their place while the driver sat at their kitchen table eating rhubarb pie. Now that would be a story to tell at school.

While they waited in the city for their second bus, people did look. But they weren't laughing. They were interested. 'You been to the trash and treasure market?' someone asked.

'No, to Grandpa's shed,' Shane replied. 'We're recycling.'

'I'd like to have a look in there,' the man said.

Another man declared, 'That's a museum piece,' and it sounded like a compliment. 'I remember them when I was your age.'

Only one said, 'Can't afford the petrol any more?' And his father stopped smiling.

'Let's eat our bush biscuits now. We've got time,' Dad said.

'Why do we need time?' For Shane, eating a biscuit was the matter of a moment, unless you were deliberately spinning it out, like chocolate biscuits.

'You'll see,' Dad grinned.

Shane took a bite. It was the hardest biscuit he'd ever bitten. 'Did GP call them iron rations because they're so hard?'

'Something like that. They're a staple food. You can go a long way on a bush biscuit.'

'Like porridge? Is that a staple food?'

Dad nodded. 'Bread, potatoes, pasta.'

'And Coco Pops are not?'

'Definitely not.'

Shane had food for thought, as he crunched through the big brown biscuit. 'Is it called a bush biscuit because it was good to have if you got lost in the bush?'

'I guess so. We always had them when we went off exploring from the farm.'

'You and Aunty Judy?'

'Yep. Bush biscuits and a billy with tea and sugar. And fishing lines of course.'

The thought of billy tea, smoky and sweet, made Shane thirsty. He'd used a lot of saliva chewing the biscuit and he was only halfway through it. 'Can we have an orange now?'

'Good idea. It'll make the bag lighter too.'

Shane felt as if there was a big rainbow inside him, coming from the pot of gold, the bag of oranges. It was the best day he'd had since . . . Since . . .

As Shane sucked his orange he noticed an old man trudging along the footpath, with a nobbly sack over his shoulder. He was wearing a checked red shirt, cheerfully patched jeans and black boots. Shane thought he looked like an out-of-season off-duty Father Christmas, with his curly white hair and his springy beard.

But it wasn't presents that were bulging his sack. It was other peoples' throw-outs. He stopped at the litter bins one after the other and rummaged through them.

Shane watched him thrust his arm right down and waited to see what he would pull out. Two drink cans. The old man stowed them in his sack. At the next bin he fished out a squashed newspaper and smoothed it carefully before adding it to his trove. Shane wondered if he needed it to look for jobs.

He waited until the old man had gone through the bin at their bus stop before he dropped in the orange skins. And he was glad he had. Because there was nothing useful there for the old man. It would have been awful, Shane thought, to be groping through other peoples' squelchy sucked orange skins for nothing.

'Father Christmas' saw Shane watching him and waiting. 'That's thoughtful of you, laddie,' he said. 'Most people wouldn't care.'

Shane dropped in the orange skins, then felt embarrassed. This old man had only a sack of other peoples' empty drink cans and he had a bag of oranges he could hardly lift. Fresh juicy oranges just picked from GP's tree. And GP digging in his beloved garden. Not scavenging through rubbish bins.

'Would you like an orange?' he asked shyly.

'Wouldn't say no!' The old man's eyes were lively with pleasure behind his well-polished glasses. He bit into the glossy skin. 'Mm, that's the ticket,' he murmured through a mouthful of juicy sweetness. 'God bless you, boy, and your family too,' he said with an understanding glance at Shane's father, standing with the old lawn-mower. 'Hard times for families, but at least you've got a family.' He shouldered his sack and went on his way. Shane wasn't sure whether he had spoken to him or his father.

Then he saw another man wandering along,

looking in the bins. He was wearing a suit, but as he got closer Shane could see it was stained and rumpled, and the shirt was grubby at the collar where the tie was pulled loose. He was carrying a briefcase, but it wasn't in good shape like the one Shane's father used to take to work. And he had a supermarket plastic bag too, hanging slack. As far as Shane could tell, it contained only a couple of empty cans.

As he shoved his hand into the bin near them, Shane could see the stubble on his face. Underneath it his skin was greeny yellow. He swore. 'Some sod has been here before me,' he grumbled. He seemed to feel Shane watching him and swung round suddenly. Shane could see

his bloodshot eyes and smell his stale breath.
It reminded him of the day after his dad
had got the sack. And it made him feel sick
and scared.

The man, who was about the same age as his
father, noticed the biscuit sticking out of Shane's
pocket. 'Give us your biscuit, son,' he said in a
rough rasping voice that didn't seem to belong
to him.

Shane pulled it from his pocket and held it
out. 'But I've eaten some of it,' he said
awkwardly.

The man grabbed it. 'Beggars can't be
choosers,' he said, and laughed hoarsely.

Shane said, 'Would you like an orange as well?'

And his father said, 'Give him two.'

'B . . . generous of you,' the man snarled at
him. 'Your turn next, mate,' he shouted in a
voice that turned to a sob, as he went off
unsteadily towards the next bin.

Shane turned to his father, sad and anxious
and angry all at once.

'Poor devil,' his father said quietly. 'Hope he
learns soon that getting shickered isn't going to
fix anything.'

Shane gripped his dad's hand, but he didn't
seem to notice. He was staring into space. 'There
but for the grace of God . . . '

'What do you mean, Dad?'

'I mean, Shane, thank God I've got you and

Shelley and your mother, to give me something to live for.'

'And GP, Dad.'

'Yeah. GP. Good old GP.' Dad grinned.

'And Bimbi.'

'Yeah, Bimbi, of course.'

Shane tried not to think of the night Dad had come home shickered and kicked the cat. He just didn't want that memory of his father.

The bus hissed to the kerb. Shane heaved his bag up. Suddenly it was heavy with redundant. But Dad didn't seem to notice. He was joking with the driver, who said, 'My dad had one of those. It's a long time since I've seen the like.' They stowed the mower and the bag and sat down.

A woman said, 'Look at that old flour bag. My mother used to make tea towels from them. Aprons too. Even bloomers when things were really tough in the Depression.'

'What are bloomers, Dad?'

'Knickers that ladies used to wear.'

'Will Mum have to make bloomers from this?'

'I hope not, Shane. But if she does, she'll make something pretty smart. Probably set a new style.'

'What's the Depression, Dad?'

'Tough times.'

'Things are really tough now, aren't they, Dad?'

'Tough enough for the time being. Until I get another job.'

Shane was silent for a moment. Then he said, 'Mum says God knows when that will be.'

His dad grinned, but not in a laughing way. 'I reckon He does too. But He's not letting on. Not just now anyway.'

At the next stop, Shane saw a house for sale. 'What's a mortgage?' he asked.

'It's a sort of loan you get from the bank, for your house.'

'Have we got one?'

'Yup.'

'But it's our house. We own it. Don't we, Dad?'

'Well . . . ' his dad said. 'Yes and no. It's our house, but we borrowed money from the bank to buy it and we've got to pay that money back.'

'When? All at once?'

'No. Just gradually. That's not so hard when you've got a job. But when you haven't . . .' his father tailed off.

'Is that why you have to sell the mower? To pay the mortgage?'

'Yep. It'll help.'

'You can have what's in my piggy bank, Dad.'

'Thanks, Shane, old man. You're a good bloke. But we'll manage without that sacrifice. You keep it for something you want, because there won't be pocket money for a while.'

'I know, Dad. We can't afford it.'

People looked as they clattered along the street from the bus stop. 'That's what's called cutting a swathe,' a man watering his garden joked.

'Setting up in antiques?' another asked.

But one man with a neglected lawn said, 'Where did you get that?'

'From Grandpa's shed,' Shane said proudly. 'We're recycling.'

'Half your luck,' he replied.

As they rattled past the broken gatepost, Tom and Jed bobbed up. 'Whatever's that?' Jed wanted to know.

'It's a lawn mower,' Shane announced.

Jed pushed Tom and they collapsed in a laughing rolling heap. 'A lawn mower! Pull the other one!' Tom's voice was muffled under Jed.

'Don't believe me then. I'll show you! Can I, Dad?'

'Go ahead, Shane.'

Shane put down his bag, took the handle, heaved the mower onto the lawn strip along the drive and pushed. The grass flew up in a thin green cloud.

'Wow!' Jed exclaimed.

'Cool!' Tom approved.

'It'd be better still if the lawn hadn't been mowed.'

'Ours hasn't been,' Jed said.

'Can we have a go?' Tom asked.

'Later,' Dad replied. 'Shane and I have things to do now.'

'Have an orange while you wait.' Shane tossed two across. 'Just picked off GP's tree.' Dumping the bag in the kitchen he announced, 'Oranges for Shelley-baby's juice, Mum. And rhubarb pie.'

'Thanks, GP,' his mum said, 'and thanks, Shane, for carrying them. Want to help make the pastry?'

'Yes please.' He especially liked rolling it out, eating the raw trimmings. 'But later, if you don't mind. Dad and I have things to do first.'

They dug a hole near the tap and Shane firmed the soil around the rhubarb crown. Dribbling water round it, he said, 'I wish we had some manure. Cow's best, GP said, but horse would do.'

'We'll have to see what we can find,' Dad said.

They dug another patch for the radishes and put in two short rows. 'Save some seed for another planting,' Dad said.

As Shane trickled them into the drill, it seemed like magic, that those tiny little dry round brown seeds would turn into crisp crunchy red radishes. He sprinkled soil over them and wished he could see through it to watch them grow.

'I've got more letters to do. So Shane's in charge,' Dad told Tom and Jed who'd been hovering nearby. 'Be careful now. Don't fiddle with the blades. Remember it's not a toy.' Shane felt as tall as the sunflower.

Six

Op Shop

On Monday his mother said, 'How you're growing, Shane.' But she didn't sound pleased. She
sounded worried. 'We'll see if we can get some
bigger clothes for you after school.'

At lunchtime an older boy hung around
Shane and his friends with a giant bag of crisps.
Shane hoped he was going to share them. But
he didn't. He just stood there, diving his hand
into the packet, cramming the golden crisps into
his mouth. The smell of them was tantalising.
Shane knew the salty taste, the crunchy feel and
his mouth watered as he watched. He took out
his orange, GP's orange, and began peeling it. The
sweet sharp scent filled his nostrils. 'I'll give you
a bit of orange for some crisps.'

'What! One section of mouldy old orange for
a couple of crisps!'

'Three segments. And it's not mouldy or old.
Grandpa picked it yesterday.'

The boy's answer was to stuff more crisps.

'Half the orange.'

At the rate he was eating he'd soon finish the packet. The boy stuffed in another handful.

'The whole orange. Peeled too.'

'Done.' The boy grabbed GP's orange, pushing the packet at Shane. It felt very light. Shane's hand went to the bottom. It was empty.

'Hey!' he shouted. 'There's none left. Give back my orange!'

But the boy was halfway across the playground. He only laughed and stuffed the orange into his mouth.

Shane felt tears of anger pricking. He threw down the empty packet and kicked it. Kicked it all the way to the bin. Then he picked it up and put it in along with the peel from the orange he'd carried home all the way from GP's. His mouth was dry. He went to the fountain for a drink. The water was tepid and tasteless. Not salty like crisps, not sweet like the orange. He swallowed his disappointment with it.

After school his mother was waiting. Shane expected to go to the supermarket but they walked another way and stopped outside an old shop which had saucepans, shoes, handbags and books in the window, a rack of clothes, a lampstand and some plants on the footpath, with a sign saying OP SHOP.

'Why are we looking here? Is it cheaper?'

'Much.' His mother manoeuvred the pusher up the step. Shane followed.

Inside it reminded him of GP's shed except that it smelled of mothballs and disinfectant with a waft of the dry scent of lavender. Old furniture, cartons of records and magazines covered the floor, shelves were crammed with ornaments and racks with clothes. His mother moved towards them. But Shane had spotted a vase rather like Grandma's. He sidled along for a closer look.

A grey-haired woman stepped out from the counter. 'Be careful. Don't touch. If you break anything you must pay for it.'

Shane stopped and stared at the vase. There were no gleaming rainbows or light fairies

50

dancing above it. But in a different place there could be. He longed to take it out into the sunshine.

He heard his mother's voice and realised she'd been calling. 'Shane, come here please and try these clothes for size.' She held an orange T-shirt. 'That looks right.'

Shane said, 'But it's not new, Mum.'

'That's why it's cheaper. Do you like the colour?'

'No. I'd rather have yellow.'

'Let's see.' She burrowed into the pile and found a yellow one with a picture of a little train and its name, Puffing Billy of the Dandenongs. 'Look. This one's never been worn, I'm sure.'

'Where's the Dandenongs, Mum?'

'Near Melbourne. Puffing Billy's a famous train, quite historic. Dad and I had a trip in it on our honeymoon.' She smiled.

Shane looked at Puffing Billy. It was neat. 'I'd like to ride in it too.'

'One day, Shane.' It was half promise, half excuse.

They chose two more T-shirts, then his mother found jeans.

'But they're not Levis, Mum. Everyone has Levis.'

'Not everyone,' she said, putting them with the T-shirts. Shane decided he would rip off the labels.

Then she found happy pants that made him think of the rainbow vase. He sidled off again. But the bossy woman was still watching, even though she was putting the clothes into a bag while calculating the price. 'I told you not to touch,' she said.

'I'm not touching,' Shane said indignantly.

'Shane,' his mother said.

'Mum, I wasn't touching, except with my eyes.' Shane was aggrieved.

'All breakages must be paid for,' the woman repeated.

'Come on, Shane,' his mother said anxiously as Shelley lunged out at a fish bowl.

Next morning Shane put on his Puffing Billy shirt. It was much more comfortable than his old tight ones. 'The Dandenongs sounds a nice place, Mum.'

'Oh, it is, Shane. We'll have a holiday there one day, p'raps.'

At recess the orange stealer sauntered across to Shane. 'Where'd you get your T-shirt?'

'My mum got it for me.'

'At the op shop, I bet.' Like Tom and Jed he seemed to know things. But he didn't know everything. 'I'll bet your mum's never been to the Dandenongs.'

'She has too,' Shane asserted.

'Anyway, that's my shirt from my gran in

Melbourne. It was too small, so my mum gave it to the op shop. Lucky for me. Kids' stuff. Puffing Billy – Thomas the Tank Engine's Australian cousin!' He swaggered off in his black Dracula T-shirt.

Shane hated the Puffing Billy T-shirt now and wanted to tear it off and throw it away. The siren went and he was glad. But in the classroom as they took out their books, a girl with six Barbie and Ken dolls asked, 'What's an op shop, Miss Williams?' And he squirmed.

She looked round. It seemed to Shane that she noticed his T-shirt. 'Oh, op shops are tops – great places where you find all sorts of interesting things,' she said. 'They're a really smart way to shop because they recycle pre-loved clothes and books and things for your house. And the money goes to good causes like Animal Welfare League and Guide Dogs for the Blind. They're an opportunity for everyone to help each other. I love them.' She touched her shining blue necklace. 'I got this at an op shop.'

After school Shane went out of his way to pass the op shop. He couldn't see the rainbow vase from the window, so he stepped just inside to look. It was still there. So was Bossy.

'You again. Tell your mother I don't like children coming here alone. You mustn't touch anything. Breakages must be paid for.'

Shane stood his ground. 'I'm not touching. I'm looking.'

Another woman, in a blue dress, came from behind the back curtain. 'Hello,' she said. 'Did you see something you want?'

'Don't encourage him,' Bossy interrupted. 'We don't want children in here.'

'You may not, but I don't mind,' the woman in blue said.

Bossy snorted and flounced behind the curtain.

The blue lady smiled at Shane. 'Can I help you?'

He pointed to the vase. 'That's like Gran's vase that got broken.'

'Is it?' she said. 'Fancy that. That was bad luck.' She lifted the vase down, dusting it with the hem of her dress. 'It's heavy. Lead crystal.'

Shane looked at it in her hands. Gran's had had stars. This had a diamond pattern. Big diamonds and little diamonds. 'There were rainbows in Gran's vase too.'

'Were there now?' said the blue lady. 'And little light fairies dancing on the ceiling?'

'Yes. That's just what we called them.'

A shaft of sunlight came through the window and a rainbow burst across the floor and lights danced up the wall.

Shane asked, 'How much is it?'

'Fifteen dollars.'

Shane stared at the rainbow on the bare boards. Fifteen dollars. How could he find that much? If only he hadn't spent Aunty Judy's birthday money. 'Fifteen dollars?'

'Yes. It's quite valuable.'

'Gran's vase was broken the night Dad got redundant,' he blurted out. And the pain was suddenly as sharp as broken glass again. He turned away. 'Put it back. I can't afford it.'

The blue lady looked at his drooping shoulders. She recognised the T-shirt. 'Wait,' she called to Shane who had already turned away. 'I'm sure we can arrange it.'

'I've got *some* money. But not fifteen dollars.'

Bossy came out. 'Still here? Does your mother know? You'd better go. Run along now.'

Shane took a last look. The sun had gone in and the rainbow and the dancing lights had disappeared. It was just a grimy dusty vase that cost fifteen dollars. 'Thank you for showing me,' he said to the blue lady and walked out.

• Seven •
Coco Pops

Next day after school his friends said, 'Stay and make up the team.' But Shane shook his head. He longed to stay and be part of the group. But he had something urgent to do. In his pocket was all the money he had – three dollars and eighty cents. He went straight to the op shop. But the rainbow vase was gone.

In its place stood an ugly purple jug. He looked above and below. Perhaps someone had moved it. But it was not there. Hand in pocket, he was turning to go when the blue lady popped out.

'Hello,' she said. 'I thought you'd be back.'

'It's gone. The rainbow vase has gone.' Shane's voice was hoarse.

'It's all right. It's safe. I've put it away for you.' She smiled.

The knot in his stomach began to loosen and he smiled back. 'Here's all the money from my piggy bank. I thought you might keep the rainbow vase until I get the rest.'

57

'I was going to suggest the same plan myself yesterday. But we got interrupted.' She winked at Shane, nodding towards the curtain.

Shane grinned, then looked serious again. 'It might take a while. I don't get pocket money now. We can't afford it. But I'll think of some way. If only I hadn't spent the birthday money from Aunty Judy. But I didn't know then. That was before Dad got redundant.'

'Of course you didn't know. Anyway, that's what birthday money is for. Don't worry. I'm sure you'll find a way. And I'll see that it doesn't get sold. Write your name and address on this card.' She wrote HOLD in red across the top, stuck it in the vase and put it away in a cupboard.

'Thank you very much. I'll be back as soon as I can.' Shane felt bubbly inside. He skipped out and hopped along the footpath, avoiding the cracks. Then he stopped. Eleven dollars and twenty cents. However could he get that?

The knot started tightening again. He suddenly wondered if his father had that feeling all the time now because of the mortgage. He was pretty sure his mother did. Put it back, we can't afford it, put it back.

He was trudging along, almost wishing he'd never seen the rainbow vase, when he came upon the supermarket trolley. Empty on its side. Right in front of him. On the footpath near a block of units. He put it upright. It still had the dollar snug in the lock. He looked around. There was nobody about. He waited a while. Nobody came. It really was abandoned. He put his bag into it, turned it round and trundled off.

It was another cranky one. No wonder who-ever took it couldn't be bothered to return it. It careered along like a rodeo bullock. Shane was sweating by the time he got it safely into the corral. Then as the dollar popped into his grasp he felt triumphant.

The checkout girl recognised him. 'Hello. You usually come Thursdays, don't you? I didn't see your mum here earlier.'

'We do come Thursdays. I just brought this trolley back because I found it.' He had a sudden thought. 'It is all right to keep the dollar, isn't it?'

'Yes, of course. And the ones from any others you find. Finders keepers,' she said. 'Are you saving up for that little car?'

Shane shook his head. 'For a present for Mum. It costs fifteen dollars.'

'Well, I reckon there's lots of trolleys out there, especially after pension days. Good luck.'

Shane ran all the way to the op shop. The lady was just bringing in the plants. 'Here you are!' Shane shouted. 'Here's a dollar.' He told her how he'd got it.

She was as pleased as he felt and entered it

on his card. 'Now you only need ten dollars twenty cents. Well done.'

Passing the church, Shane decided to go in and tell the lady how much he'd enjoyed the chocolate biscuits. She was not there. But in the porch was a big carton labelled: FOR THOSE FAMILIES WHO CAN'T AFFORD. And right on top Shane could see a packet of Coco Pops. A large packet.

It seemed specially for him. It didn't feel quite right to take it without asking. But the label seemed to say it was. He waited a while, hoping the lady would come. But she didn't.

He looked at the packet longingly. He could almost taste the Coco Pops. Surely they were

meant for him. The lady knew he liked them and she probably thought too, that he'd be back. But Mum would be wondering where he was. He couldn't wait much longer.

He picked up the packet. It felt so light. He wrote THANK YOU FOR THE COCO POPS on a piece of paper, printed his name and address underneath and left it on the carton.

When he put the packet on the table his mother said, 'Why were you so long? And where did you get that?'

'From the church.'

'Did the lady give it to you?'

'Not exactly. But she knows I like them.'

'Did you take it without asking? Oh Shane, that's stealing. You must go and put it back straightaway.'

'But Mum, the label on the box says the things are for families who can't afford them.'

'Maybe. But you shouldn't have taken it without asking. Take it back now. At once. And tell the lady you're sorry.'

Shane was thirsty. But his mother was so upset he didn't dare stop for a drink. His legs were aching and his shoes were tight. It seemed a long way back. The Coco Pops, feather-light on the way home, now felt heavy with guilt and shame. And his stomach felt all wormy squirmy at the thought of seeing the lady. He hoped she wouldn't be there and that he could just slip them back, grab his message and run. As he approached he held the packet behind him.

But she was there. 'Hello, Shane. You are Shane, aren't you? And you found the Coco Pops!'

Shane felt his face going hot and red. 'Mum sent me. I'm sorry I took them.' He thrust the packet at her.

'Keep them, Shane. They're your favourite. That's why I got them.'

But Shane shook his head. 'Mum was mad at me for taking them. She said I stole them. I didn't mean to. I just thought . . . '

'Well, let's see what we can find that your mother *would* like,' the friendly lady said. 'What do you have for breakfast now?'

'Porridge.'

'Then here's the very thing.' She produced a big packet of rolled oats.

Shane swallowed hard. 'Thank you,' he managed to say.

'You don't like porridge?'

Shane shook his head. 'No, but Dad does. And Mum says it gives him a good start for the day when he goes job hunting.'

'It does too. She's quite right. It's hard work job hunting. It takes a lot of energy. What about some brown sugar? That's good with porridge. And do you like sultanas?'

Shane nodded. 'Mum used to put them in my lunch box.'

She put a packet beside the sugar and rolled oats. 'Try some in your porridge too. You'll like it. And you could make Anzacs for your school lunch. I expect your mother's got the recipe. If she hasn't, I'll bring it next week.'

'Do you think God's going to tell about Dad's job soon? Dad's given up smoking because we can't afford it.'

'God helps those who help themselves,' the lady said, more to herself than Shane. He was puzzled. After all he'd helped himself to the Coco Pops and he'd had to give them back. Lots of things were hard to understand now Dad was redundant.

• Eight •
Trolley Spotter

On Thursday the supermarket checkout girl said, 'Hello, Shane. The manager would like to see you and your mother.'

His mother looked anxious. 'Oh Shane, what have you done? You haven't stolen anything, have you? Or broken something?'

Shane felt mad. 'No, Mum. Of course I haven't.' Why did everyone keep accusing him of breaking things? All the same he felt a bit nervous.

The manager came out smiling. 'Hello, Shane. Mrs Clark, I want to compliment you on your son's helpfulness and honesty. It doesn't happen very often that anyone returns a trolley. We'll give you two dollars, Shane, for every trolley you find and bring back.'

'You mean as well as the one in the trolley?'

The manager smiled again. 'Yes. And here's two dollars for yesterday's.'

'What about the ones in peoples' yards.

64

That'd be trespassing to get them, wouldn't it?'

'Yes. Leave them to us. Just give us the address and we'll give you a dollar each for them too. We'd be very grateful. We're losing more and more even though it costs people a dollar each time. If that's all right with you, Mrs Clark?'

She nodded.

'Thanks, Shane. We'll be seeing you.'

Shane said, 'You take Shelley, Mum. I'll push the trolley.' They set off down the long aisle. Now he really understood it was a campaign to beat the mortgage, spotting the best value, getting the most for the money, made him feel good. 'Look, a kilo of this brand for the same price as 750 grams of that,' he pointed out. 'And there – three litres the same price as two.'

When they came to the biscuits, Shane didn't pause. 'We can make our own, Mum. Anzacs they're called, the church lady said.'

'Anzacs!' Mum smiled. 'Gran made them. They're yummy. We'll make some tonight. We'll need golden syrup.'

Passing the cordials she said, 'And Gran always made cordial. We'll just need citric acid and lemon essence.'

Shane slowed down at the ice blocks. Just hoping.

Mum remembered, 'We made ice blocks from our own cordial, so let's do that too.'

Walking home she nearly spoiled everything.

65

She said, 'That was good about returning the trolley. What have you done with the dollar?'

'That's a secret, Mum.'

They walked a bit further without talking, then she said, 'I don't think I like secrets like that. Not secrets about money.'

You and Dad have secrets from me, Shane thought resentfully. But he only said, 'Don't ask, Mum. You'll like this one.'

As they weighed sugar and measured water for the cordial, she said, 'I wish we had some lemons. It tastes so much better.'

'There's some on Tom and Jed's tree. I'll ask. We'll give them ice blocks.' He came back with Tom, Jed and three lemons. They washed them, grated the rinds, squeezed and strained the juice.

'Smells good, doesn't it?' said Jed, puckering his mouth.

Carefully they poured the boiling water over the snowy mountain, watching it melt away. They took turns stirring until the last grains dissolved.

'In with the lemon now,' Mum said.

The steaming syrup went cloudy, tinged greenish yellow. They breathed in the smell. 'Makes you thirsty, doesn't it?' Tom exclaimed. 'We don't have to wait till it's cool, do we?'

'No,' Mum said. 'And you need less than bought cordial.' They each put a spoonful into a tall glass, filled it with iced water and sipped.

'Better than that shop stuff,' Jed declared.

Shane knew it was so long since Jed had had cordial, he'd almost forgotten the taste. But he agreed. It was sweet yet tangy. They washed their glasses and Mum said, 'Come back later. We're making Anzacs.'

It was good drooling the golden syrup into the rolled oats, making little balls, spacing them on the trays. 'Leave plenty of room,' Mum advised. 'It's amazing how they spread.'

They took turns scraping the bowl and Shane gave Shelley a taste too. Then they crouched in front of the oven door, sniffing the golden smell, watching the biscuits spread into big brown circles. 'This is better than watching TV,' Jed said. Shane knew Tom and Jed didn't have TV any more.

Tom said, 'I hope they cook quickly. The smell makes you hungry.'

Shane knew Tom was always hungry.

Mum announced, 'You can take them out now. Just wait another minute. Then they'll be crisp and crunchy.'

Shane turned over Grandma's egg timer. It was more fun than the stove timer. They watched the sand trickle through grain by grain. 'Now!' they shouted together.

'Only two each. They've got to last,' Shane's mum said.

Stringy Jed and even stringier Tom agreed, 'We know.'

• Nine •
Magic Eyes

Shane's dad woke him early on Saturday morning. 'We're going fishing.'

Shane hopped out of bed. 'I'll put your rod in the car.'

'I'm selling the rod. And we're not going in the car.'

Selling the fishing rod? Shane wondered if he was really awake. The rod was his father's pride and joy. Not going in the car?

'We'll put a notice about the rod in the newsagent's, then catch the bus to GP's. He's got some old lines. Mum's made us lunch.'

The porridge was bubbling on the stove. Shane took a bigger serve than usual. It was nice with sultanas. And the brown sugar was good too. He'd have to choose. Dad was trickling golden syrup over his. 'Can I do that?'

'Sure. Looks good, tastes good.'

Shane trickled the slow-flowing syrup in patterns.

'Don't take too long. We've got a bus to catch,' Dad reminded him.

While Dad was looking through the fishing gear Shane followed GP down the rows of vegetables to get worms. 'I'll spare you a few out of the compost.' Underneath the rotting vegetable scraps and brown damp weeds GP uncovered a mass of pink shiny wriggling earthworms.

He gloated. 'Beautiful, aren't they? Look how they've turned the rubbish into humus.' He crumbled it lovingly between his gnarled hands. 'We'll get good tomatoes out of this, you'll see.' He scooped up some worms into a margarine container. 'The fish won't be able to resist these fellas.'

They picked oranges. 'Not too many,' GP said. 'Got to leave room in the sack for the catch.' He pulled a handful of young carrots, and washed them under the tap. 'Take these, young rabbit. For your lunch.'

Going to the beach Shane said, 'Why haven't we got a vegetable garden?'

His dad didn't answer for a moment. Then he replied slowly, 'Because I've been too lazy, I suppose. Played too much golf.'

They walked out to the end of the jetty, crunching crushed cockle shells and dried sea-weed, avoiding seagull splats. The sea was spark-ling blue, rippled by a light breeze. 'That's good,'

Dad said. 'The fish won't see the line.'

Several people were already fishing. Shane peered into their buckets. Fish were still flip-flopping in some, but in others they were lying stiff and stary-eyed. Some people were baiting hooks with cockles, others were using maggots.

Shane and his dad chose their spot so the wind was behind them and the sun wasn't in their eyes. 'The hooks are a bit rusty, but I don't think the fish'll mind. All they'll see is the worm.' They dropped their lines over and settled to wait. It wasn't long before Shane felt a tug. He jerked the line and started pulling it in. Suddenly it went slack and light.

'Bad luck. And he took your worm, the blighter.'

Shane baited up again. He hoped they'd catch some fish, but even if they didn't, it was good just to sit, legs dangling, listening to Dad joking and yarning with the other men.

Some kids in smart clothes came along with their parents, holding packages of fish and chips. They sat down to eat. Shane watched the crisp brown batter, the fat gold chips disappearing. Then suddenly they'd had enough and started tossing the chips, the delectable desirable scrumptious chips, to the seagulls hovering overhead in a squawking squabbling cloud. A specially greedy gull flew off with the last chip while the boys crumpled the empty paper, tossing it aside.

'Better than putting the chips in the bin,' Dad said. Shane hadn't realised he'd been watching too. 'At least we had a good show with the gulls. And they should be too full to hang around us with their beady eyes on our lunch. So we can enjoy it in peace.' He unwrapped the sandwiches. 'White bread again,' he said in disgust. 'Why do we always have white bread now?'

'Because it's cheaper, Dad, especially when it's on special. It's nearly a dollar cheaper then than wholemeal.' Privately Shane thought the change to white bread was the one big improvement in the money-saving shopping campaign.

But Dad obviously didn't. 'It's time we made our own. I saw the old tins today in GP's shed. We'll get them next week and give it a go.'

They caught six fish. 'Two feeds, Dad.'

'Yep. If we have a good pile of chips, one each will do. And I've been thinking about what you said. We must get a vegie garden going. We'll need plenty of spuds for all the fish we'll catch.'

That evening, full and contented, Shane was ready to settle in front of the TV. But Dad called him outside. He was walking round the back yard. 'Just thinking where we'll grow our 'taters. We'll pull up the pavers.'

'Pull up the pavers? But we only laid them last year!'

'True,' Dad said. 'But it's the best place. The spuds'll get plenty of sun there. We'll do it tomorrow. And we can sell the pavers. They'll bring in a handy sum.'

They started next morning. Shane was a bit sorry. It was a good spot for hopscotch and bouncing a ball. But Dad said, 'It's something for nothing. Potatoes'll grow from eyes. I saved last night's peelings from the chips Mum did. That's a start. And there'll be more tonight.'

Tom and Jed looked over the fence to see what was happening. They called Shane across. 'Your dad gone bonkers? Pulling up all that paving you just had done!'

'No, he's fine. We're planting potatoes.'

Tom and Jed looked at each other, wiggling their fingers on their foreheads.

'I know where there are more peelings, Dad.' He burrowed in the bin, hauling out bundles of kitchen scraps. 'Found some!' he shouted triumphantly. 'And here's more!'

Tom and Jed looked across again. 'You gone bonkers too?'

'Nope. Potatoes'll grow from peelings. Doesn't cost a cent to plant them.'

Tom climbed the fence. 'I'll help your dad while you look in our bin too. Pass it over, Jed.'

The smell from the bins made Shane say, 'We should use the other scraps for compost, Dad.'

'Good idea. But for a start we'll dig everything

into the ground to get the garden going. So see what you can find.'

By the time he and Jed had sorted all the bundles, Dad and Tom had lifted and stacked a section of pavers. 'Jed and I'll carry on with Tom, Dad, while you start digging.' Shane could hardly wait to get the potato eyes bedded safely in the earth to start growing. He'd have to teach Shelley not to pull them up.

'Like to turn the first sod?' Dad handed him the spade. Shane drove it through the soft sand into the soil. 'Go, 'taties, go!'

'Can I?' asked Tom.

'Me too,' said Jed.

'We'll have a potato feast with our first harvest,' Dad promised. 'Bake them in the barbecue.'

Prising, levering and stacking the pavers was warm work. Shane was glad Shelley was inside asleep and not underfoot. Everyone was pleased when Shane's mum came out with glasses of cordial. He said, 'What about our ice blocks?'

'When you're finished?' she suggested.

'A celebration,' Shane said.

They returned to work, tearing up pavers, breaking up ground beneath. As the spade jarred against the hard earth, Dad said, 'Spuds will help break up the soil. It's marvellous the way they do.'

Shane banged at the clods. It was so different

75

from GP's soft crumbly soil. He looked at the little potato eyes on the shrivelling peel and wondered how they could survive, let alone grow and turn into potatoes for mashing and frying and baking. He hoped his dad was right after all that work wrecking the patio. They must be magic eyes.

Finally the last paver was stacked, the last little curl of peel planted. Shane, Tom and Jed took turns watering them in, then sucked their ice blocks.

'Not bad,' said Tom. 'We'll have to make some.'

'And plant spuds too,' Jed said.

• Ten •
Mucking Out

On Monday morning Shane called, 'Hey, Mum, that's queer. No milk. And some dog must've taken the paper.'

'No, Shane. We've cut out deliveries.'

'Will we fetch them ourselves?'

'Well, powdered milk.'

'Because it's cheaper.' Shane knew.

Mum nodded, filling a jug with water and adding white powder. 'You can beat it.' He whisked till it frothed, just like milk from the cow he'd seen at a dairy. He decided it might be more fun, even if it didn't taste quite the same.

Dad came to the table. It seemed strange to see him with nothing to read. 'Aren't we getting the paper any more, Dad? What about the cricket and the footy pictures?'

'You can see them on TV.'

'But I can't cut them out to pin up. And how will you find out about jobs?'

'I can read it free at the library. And the price

buys a stamp and some envelopes. We must think of these things, Shane.'

Shane wondered what he could think of. But as he walked home that afternoon, all he could think of were his tight shoes.

The mail box was empty, but Dad was home and Shane saw crumpled envelopes in the waste-paper basket. That's where all the letters ended up. It was rotten for Dad writing so many and only getting answers that were no good.

'You're limping, Shane,' Mum observed. 'What happened?'

'I'm not, Mum. Nothing's happened.' But when he took off his shoes and saw the blisters, he knew he mustn't mention them.

On Thursday in the supermarket shoe section his mother paused, 'How much of Aunty Judy's birthday money is left?'

'None, Mum. I spent it on model cars. Don't you remember?'

She nodded. 'Yes, of course I do now. Silly of me.'

'Anyway these aren't Reeboks,' Shane said.

They passed the cat food. He stopped. 'Bimbi's tucker, Mum, don't forget.

'No, Shane. She must learn to eat porridge.'

'Oh, poor Bimbi, Mum!' But she ignored him.

On his trolley trip he called to see the lady at church. 'Next week we're getting the tins from GP's shed and Dad'll make bread.'

'Home-made bread is super. Just as well you came. I've got the very thing.' From the back of the cupboard she brought out a big pack. 'Special breadmaking flour. Sure it's not too heavy?'

''Course not. Thanks. Dad'll be pleased.'

Shane could hardly wait for Saturday. Not far from GP's they passed the racecourse and saw horses training. 'There might be some manure there, Dad, for the rhubarb.' But his father didn't seem to hear.

'You get the worms,' GP told Shane, 'and you get the bread tins,' he told his dad, 'while I get the Milo.'

'Drink up, Shane. You've given me an idea. We've got something else to do,' Dad said.

They'd only gone two stops on the bus when he stood to get off.

'Quick.' They turned into a side street. 'There's stables along here. They might give us manure. Probably glad to get rid of it.'

After three blocks they came to one. 'Let's give it a try.' They went in, their sack of bread tins clanking.

'Need any manure cleared out?' Dad asked the man currycombing a horse.

'Sure do. You're a godsend. Thought I'd have to do it myself. Our regular's on holidays and our relief just rang in sick. You can have it if you clear it all out.'

79

Shane felt excited. But his father wasn't. 'What's the pay?'

'Pay? You're getting the manure.'

'But you'd have paid the other fellow,' his father said.

The man looked him up and down. 'Out of work?'

Shane's dad nodded.

'You've got a cheek, haven't you? But I like it. Twenty bucks if you come again tomorrow and don't let me down.'

'It's on. Shane, go back to GP's for the old cart.'

'Can't you get the car, Dad?'

'Not now. When a stable needs mucking out,

it needs mucking out.' He rolled up his sleeves. 'Show me the shovel and where to start.'

Shane hurried. 'Forgotten something?' GP asked.

'No. We're getting manure at a stable. Dad asked for the cart.'

'Mucking out, is he? Good old Mike. I'll give a hand.'

Together they trundled the cart along. It ran much more smoothly than a trolley but it was heavy. Shane was glad GP was helping. 'Pity we didn't have time to oil the wheels,' GP said. 'She's making a bit of a racket. They ought to hear us coming.'

Dad had cleared several stalls of straw and manure. 'We've got a couple of cartloads there, young rabbit. Sweated labour, but it'll make the vegies grow.'

Three trips they made. The man was impressed. 'You're a good team,' he said, eyeing GP's muscly arms and swinging style with the shovel. 'I'd be glad of your help again. I'll put you in my book and if there's an emergency I'll ring you. See you tomorrow.'

The last trip seemed a long way, even with Dad pushing. They ate their fishing lunch on GP's verandah, then bagged up the manure. Shane was tired.

'Stay the night here,' GP suggested. 'It's chops for tea.'

Shane was tempted by the thought of a juicy brown chop. Mum always cooked pasta now. But GP's house smelled funny. And though he didn't smell too good himself with manure on his clothes, he said, 'Thanks GP, but I think I'd better go home. Mum'd miss me. So would Shelley-baby. And Bimbi.'

Bimbi always waited for him. Always on the gatepost when he came home. She'd be waiting there now probably, ready to leap down and run to him. Shane loved the feel of her rubbing round his legs and the softness of her fur and the way she vibrated when she jumped purring into his arms.

His dad said, 'We'll be back tomorrow, Dad. Early.'

'You won't catch me napping,' GP said. 'I'll be ready.'

Next morning Shane woke to a wonderful smell. At first he thought he was dreaming. Then he realised that he wasn't and that it was the smell of baking bread. He ran to the kitchen. Dad was just pulling two loaves out of the oven, high tops golden brown.

'Still too hot to eat,' he said. 'We'll take a loaf to GP.'

• Eleven •
Bimbi

On Monday Shane went home a different way, looking for trolleys. Passing a park he noticed cans lying on the grass. That's what he could do. Collect cans. They were worth money. He stuffed them into his school-bag, wondering where to find more.

The sports oval. Sure to be plenty in those bins. He found so many he had to crush them to fit them all in and while he was stamping he didn't notice some older boys approaching.

Suddenly they surrounded him. 'You little rat. Stealing our cans. This is our territory. We'll teach you.'

Shane looked up at their menacing faces and felt panic. They meant trouble. And there were four of them. Big and bullying. He tried to bolt. But they seized him, yanking the bag from his grip, twisting off the handle, tipping out the contents. 'Ours, see! You just leave well alone!'

'I didn't get them all here,' Shane protested. 'I got some in the park.'

'Our territory too. Get lost or you'll be sorrier than this.'

Two boys up-ended him into the bin. His face went into greasy pie wrappers, smelly scraps and broken bottles. He flailed wildly, but they still had hold of his legs. It seemed an age before they suddenly let him go. He could hear them running off laughing as he clawed his way out, dirty, bruised and bleeding.

He picked up the empty bag with its useless handle and trailed miserably home. Tom and Jed saw him. 'Who's been roughing you up?' Shane explained. 'We can all do with some money,' they said. 'We'll be our own gang, find our own territory. Better come and get cleaned up before your mum sees you. Then we'll tell her.'

His mother was shocked at his cut face and scratched hands, his torn shirt and broken bag. 'Shane, I've told you. You're to come straight home after school.'

'But Mum, I can earn money collecting cans,' he protested.

Tom and Jed asserted, 'He'll be okay, Mrs Clark. We're going together in future. Nobody will take *us* on.'

Shane heard his parents discussing it that night. 'You've got to let him, Jen,' Dad said. 'You can't mollycoddle him. Times are tough. Other kids have to do it.'

So every day after school Shane went off, sometimes with Tom and Jed for cans, sometimes alone scouting for trolleys. He often longed to stay and join in a game with his friends. But he tried to avoid them. He didn't want them to know. And every day his shoes hurt more. So he took them off, tied the laces and hung them round his neck, stopping to put them back on just before he got home. But one day he forgot. Then the trouble began. When his mother saw him barefooted she became upset.

'I was just trying to save them, Mum, so they don't get worn out.' But Shane couldn't fool her.

'They're too tight. You're needing a new pair.'

That night he heard his parents arguing. 'Shane must have new shoes.'

'Kids do go without them. We did on the farm.'

'On the farm! Twenty years ago. Besides Shelley should have sandals too now she's almost walking.'

'Well, what about the twenty dollars from mucking out?'

'Twenty dollars! He wants Reeboks.'

'I'll sell my guitar.'

'What's the use of saying that? No one's bought your golf clubs or fishing rod or the pavers yet.'

'We need an ad in the paper.'

'You know we can't afford that, Mike.'

'The mucking-out money then. And I'll get the dole soon, then it'll be better.'

'We could go to the Salvos.'

His father exploded. 'Go to the Salvos? Go to the Salvos!' Then there was the sound of crying again. And it was the sound of his father.

Shane pulled the doona over his head. The Salvos?

Next day was Thursday. His mother headed off in hat and dark glasses. 'Where are you going, Mum?' It was not towards the supermarket.

'To the Salvos. To get food.'

'For nothing?'

His mother nodded but wouldn't talk.

Other families were waiting at the place with the big red shield on the window which said THE SALVATION ARMY – THE FAMILY PLACE. Other women were wearing dark glasses too and they all seemed to hang their heads. Shane watched the Salvation Army people. They looked like soldiers in their neat uniforms. But friendly soldiers, brisk, kind, patting Shelley, smiling at Shane, handing out tins of baked beans, spaghetti, plum jam and more baked beans. No guns anywhere. Just smiles. And baked beans.

The plastic bag bumped sharp with edges against his legs and hung heavy, cutting his fingers. Shane longed for a trolley, even a cranky one. But they didn't find one.

His mother had gone very quiet. When they got home she said to his father, 'Baked beans tonight for a change.' Shane knew it was meant to sound cheerful. But somehow it didn't.

Dad said, 'I've spent the mucking-out money on an ad. And I'm starting a lawnmowing round.' He showed them the leaflet he'd printed.

LAWNS MOWED THE ENVIRONMENTALLY FRIENDLY WAY!
GOOD OLD-FASHIONED VALUE WITH A HAND MOWER.
RING MIKE FOR FREE QUOTE AND SMILING SERVICE.

'That's great, Dad! I'll stick them in letter-boxes. And good luck with the ad.'

On Friday afternoon Shane trudged street after street putting leaflets into letterboxes. And found two trolleys. He raced to the supermarket and collected his money just before it closed. Too late for the op shop. But the rainbow vase was almost paid for now. He hurried home, forgetting his shoes around his neck again.

Bimbi wasn't waiting at the gate. He called. But she didn't come.

He asked Tom and Jed. 'Seen Bimbi?'

'Nope. Probably having her tea.'

He ran inside. 'Bimbi! Where's Bimbi?'

His parents both spoke at once. 'She ran

away,' his mother said, pressing Shelley close to
her chest.

'She was run over,' his father said.

Shane stared at them both, his heart pound-
ing. 'Bimbi! It's not true! You're both telling lies,'
he shouted. 'Where is she? Bimbi, Bimbi,' he
called desperately, hoping to see her uncurl from
a corner, stretch and come running to him. 'Bimbi!'

His parents stood like strangers, staring at
each other. Silent. Like statues. Stone. Or ice.
His mother began to cry. Shelley-baby whim-
pered. His father said gruffly, 'Sorry, Shane.'

'Sorry! What for?' Shane shouted. 'You've sold
her!' He didn't want to believe it. But he knew
it was true. 'You've sold her! Sold Bimbi! How

could you? How could you? Bimbi . . . ' and his voice was a wail.

'You don't tell me things. You don't explain,' he shouted. 'You accuse me of having secrets. But mine was a good secret.' If he'd had the rainbow vase now, he would have thrown it on the floor to smash into a myriad fragments. Instead he threw down the trolley dollars. 'I hate you both. *I hate you!*'

His parents both started to speak at once. 'You need shoes and I knew you'd set your heart on Reeboks,' his mother said.

Shane hurled his outgrown shoes across the room. 'You sold Bimbi! For Reeboks!'

'We didn't advertise Bimbi, Shane. We never thought of selling her. But nobody was interested in any of the things I did advertise,' his father said. 'There wasn't a taker even for the computer or the guitar. But the last person liked Bimbi. He knows about Persians. She's gone to a good home.'

'She had a good home here!' Shane choked back a sob and ran out. He slammed his door and dragged his desk against it, then flung himself on the bed. Bimbi, Bimbi. Nothing could hold back his tears. And no plea from his parents would make him open the door.

On Saturday morning his mother said apologetically, 'We'll choose your shoes this morning.

89

And you must keep your money for your secret.'

'I won't wear shoes bought with Bimbi! I'd sooner go barefoot for ever.' Though he was starving, Shane shoved away his porridge, grabbed his dollars and ran out of the house.

Tom and Jed saw him. 'Trouble?'

'They've sold Bimbi.'

'Bimbi! They've sold Bimbi? Oh no,' said Jed.

'TV, computer, car. But not Bimbi,' said Tom. 'Bimbi . . . ' and Tom gave a sob he didn't even bother to try turning into a cough.

'How could they?' Jed asked.

Jed and Tom hadn't had a pet since their dog died two years ago. Suddenly Shane knew why Jed was always watching birds, snails, lizards, grasshoppers, and why Tom always picked up Bimbi every chance he got. They stood a moment in silence, knowing that the soft purring little pussy was no longer there to comfort them.

'Pity she was a pedigree Persian,' Jed said. 'If she'd been an ordinary moggie nobody would have offered megabucks for her.'

'And megabucks would be pretty hard for your parents to refuse right now,' Tom said. Always practical and always hungry, Tom looked at Shane. 'You had breakfast?'

Shane shook his head.

'Come on. We'll get some chips. Then we'll go for cans.'

Shane didn't let himself wonder where Tom

and Jed got the money. He just sat between them, grateful they were beside him, grateful for the parcel warm on his knees, and the hot filling chips.

They stayed out all day and made a good haul, scouting round the shopping centre, car parks and a more distant oval. Shane used his trolley reward for pies and drinks. But when they got home he realised with an empty feeling that Bimbi would never be there again to meet him.

But tonight GP was. 'Hello, young rabbit. I've brought you a surprise. Come and look.' On the back lawn a little fowl run had sprung up and four bantams were pecking contentedly. 'What are you going to call them?'

'Oh, GP! Are they all for me?'

'Yep. Shelley's too young to look after bantams yet. But she'll enjoy watching yours and eating their eggs.'

Shane felt his heart go out to the little brown hens. He still felt sick with longing for Bimbi. Nothing could ever take her place, of course. But it wouldn't be so lonely now. He hugged GP, who said over the top of his head to nobody in particular, 'A boy's got to have a creature to love.' Then to Shane, 'We'll fix up a bit of a house for them tomorrow.'

Good as his word, GP was back on Sunday morning with a bundle of old planks, hammer and nails, and two wooden boxes. With help from Tom and Jed, the bantams soon had a neat little house complete with nesting boxes. Then the boys went off on their can round again.

In the evening when they got home, GP had gone. So had the TV. Lying in bed in the quiet house, Shane wondered where Bimbi was. If only someone had bought the TV first. If only he hadn't spent all his birthday money. He'd wanted the model cars so much. He stared at them on the shelf. Useless stupid things. Now he only wanted Bimbi, warm and alive, curled up beside him. If only . . .

On Monday after collecting, Jed asked, 'Can we come and watch TV?'

'It's gone,' Shane muttered. Nobody mentioned Bimbi.

'Car next,' Tom said. 'See ya.'

On Tuesday they went for shoes. 'Only money from the TV. And we'll go to the op shop,' Shane declared. 'I don't care if they're smelly and scruffy. I don't care.'

His mother objected. But he didn't budge. 'If you buy new ones I won't wear them. I just won't,' he shouted. He still couldn't face the thought of Bimbi being sold for shoes. He'd never be able to face it. How could he ever forgive his parents? He was still raging at their betrayal. 'I'll wear secondfoot shoes that stink.'

'Let's all go to the op shop,' his father suggested. 'Who knows what we might find!'

They found a pair of pre-loved sneakers that were Shane's size and hardly shabby at all. And they were Reeboks. Shane walked home without limping. With his toes almost singing in their new space.

To find a new shock.

• Twelve •
Mortgagee Auction

The red Ford was still in the carport. But a sign
next door announced the house was for auction.
Mortgagee auction. Tom and Jed's house.

His mother hurried inside with Shelley, without comment. But Shane stood staring at it.
Reading the words which spelled out uprooting
for Tom and Jed, and the end of a friendship he'd always known. He couldn't even begin
to think what it would be like not having
Tom and Jed next door. Teasing, taunting Tom,
thoughtful Jed. Making fun of him because
he was younger. But always standing up for
him against others, protecting him, teaching
him. Like big brothers.

Shane felt bereft at the prospect of their
going. And now there was no Bimbi for comfort.
He was still standing, staring, silent, numb with
loneliness, when Tom and Jed appeared. They
all stared at each other. For a moment there
were no words.

Then Tom blurted out, 'Our old man's cleared out.'

'Gone interstate looking for a job,' Jed added.

'Not coming back,' Tom said.

'Mum won't have him back,' Jed added.

'He's been knocking her about,' Tom said and his voice was hoarse.

'Beat her up proper yesterday before he left.' Jed choked on the words and the memory.

Shane thought of the day his father had come home redundant. He remembered him pushing his mother out of the way so he could go to the pub. He remembered his mother falling and the angry mark across her cheek and forehead. He looked from Tom to Jed and back. All Tom's bravado had gone. Know-it-all swaggering Tom was stripped, shaken. Icy cold inside, Shane knew. And there wasn't even Bimbi any more for him to hold, for warmth against the hurt.

He looked again at Jed. Jed, who'd rescued kittens from a drain and reported a man to the RSPCA for beating a dog. Jed, who didn't have a dog any more, though every dog wanted to be his friend.

Shane felt as if a hundred rainbow vases had shattered around them, making them fearful to stir a step to find a way through the senseless pain lying in wait whichever way they turned.

If only Bimbi . . . But there were the bantams now, GP's bantams, his bantams he hadn't named yet. 'Come and see how the bantams have settled in,' he said. 'Maybe they've started laying.'

They walked past the stacked pavers nobody had bought, past the neat rows of potatoes shooting strong and green through their mulch of manure, past thrusting rhubarb and sprouting radishes.

The four little bantams ran clucking to greet them.

'What have you called them?' Tom asked.

'These two are Thomasina and Jedda,' Shane said on the spur of the moment. 'I haven't thought of names for the others. Can you?'

'Bimbi,' said Tom at once.

'Brown Beauty,' said Jed, who'd been reading about the famous black horse.

'And look!' Shane exclaimed. 'You little rippers! Four eggs!' They took turns holding the four little eggs, smooth, warm and dusky brown. 'Take them home for tea,' he said, feeling desolate again for Tom and Jed, and seeing in a sudden burst as clear and bright as the rainbow from the vase, all he had to be grateful for, all he had to share. He certainly could afford to be generous, even with the very first precious eggs from his bantams.

That night, after more Salvation Army baked beans, he apologised. 'I'm sorry I said that the other night. I don't hate you, Dad. And I don't hate you, Mum. I just hate what you did.'

'We hate what we did too, Shane,' Mum admitted, hugging him. 'And we hate ourselves for doing it.'

'And we hate all that's happened that forced us to sell Bimbi,' Dad added. 'So many things have gone wrong in Australia and people like you and Mum and Shelley have to pay for other peoples' mistakes and greed.'

'You too, Dad. And Tom and Jed.'

'And their mum and dad,' Mum said quietly.

Shane was suddenly pierced by a new fear closer to home. Just across the table. 'Promise you won't walk out on us, Dad.'

'I'd never do that, Shane.'

'Promise you won't go interstate looking for a job.'

'Not unless I can take you all with me,' Dad replied.

Shane believed him. Promise you won't hit Mum or Shelley. Or me, because you can't find a job, Shane wanted to add. But he looked at Dad carefully, noticing his curly black hair going grey at the forehead, and his eyes, crinkly at the corners from laughing, with no smile in them. And he couldn't say it. He knew Dad wouldn't do it again.

He looked at his mum. Her hair, always so pretty, wavy gold, was straggly and lank, not shiny any more. And her brown eyes were as dull and dark as GP's rooms. But he still loved her and maybe the rainbow vase would make the light dance in them again. For a moment he regretted the pies and drinks. Then he thought of Tom and Jed. There wouldn't be pies, drinks or chips for them now.

Over the next week he prowled tirelessly for trolleys. Only three more and he would be carrying home the vase. He found two. But looking for the last one was like throwing the dice for the exact winning number. He walked and walked, grateful for the secondfoot sneakers, hoping at every corner to see the one he needed.

On Friday he found it.

He noticed an old woman having difficulties

with the trolley she was pushing home. She was small and frail, and he felt sorry for her. So he ran up and said, 'Like a hand? I'm pretty good at trolleys.'

'Thanks, young fella. You'll need to be good to keep this one under control. It's a fair camel. I feel like a circus act. I don't know why they don't do something at the supermarket about them.'

She was right. It was a camel. Contrary and cantankerous. Shane thought it was probably the same one they'd first taken home. Or its cousin. It needed all his skill to coax and cajole it along without skittling the old lady. He hoped she didn't live too far away.

He was sweating and almost breathless before she slowed down and said, 'Here we are. Come on in. I'm dying for a cuppa and you must be too.'

Shane helped carry the shopping into her cheery kitchen. He would have loved to stay and chat. She reminded him of GP. But he said, 'Thanks. I'd better not. But I'll take the trolley back if you like.'

'I certainly would. Thanks very much. And keep the dollar. You've earned it.'

As he wrestled the stupid trolley to the super-market, he agreed heartily with the old lady. They should do something about them. And it gave him an idea. 'I've got it! My last one! Can I see the manager?' he said to the checkout girl, who was almost as excited as he was.

'I'll buzz him for you,' she offered.

Shane said to him, 'That's six trolleys I've brought back. But it's no wonder people don't bother. They really are a menace. A poor old lady was having terrible trouble this afternoon. You ought to get them fixed. My Dad's good at fixing things.'

The manager smiled at him. 'You're right, Shane. Customer relations. Tell your dad to come and see me. And here's a bonus for you.' He gave Shane three extra dollars.

Shane panted into the op shop just as the blue lady was bringing in the sign. 'Congratulations, Shane. I knew you would do it.' She wrapped the vase and put it in a plastic bag. 'Now watch where you're walking and don't trip.'

Shane wished there was time to show his church friend, but it was too late. Besides, he couldn't wait to get home. He washed the vase carefully in the bathroom and dried it on his towel before re-wrapping it and putting it on the table at Mum's place.

'What's this? A celebration?' Dad asked. 'Pasta! With bacon!' They'd been having baked beans and soup from GP's vegetables for almost two weeks.

Mum said, 'Someone rang to collect the pavers tomorrow. The first dole cheque's come. You got your first mowing job.'

'And if you go to see the manager at the super-market tomorrow, he'll give you a job fixing the trolley wheels,' Shane announced importantly. 'It's all arranged.'

Dad grinned at him crookedly and tousled his hair. 'So who bought the present?' he asked.

'I did,' said Shane. 'With trolley dollars.' And watching Mum's face as she unwrapped it, he felt like the sunflower again.

'Oh, Shane, so that was your secret,' was all she could say. But her hug said everything. They made a ceremony after tea, carrying it to the hall table. Shelley laughed and reached for the fairy lights.

'Mustn't touch, Shelley,' Shane warned. 'Very precious. Mummy's special vase. Tomorrow you'll see the fairies again. But they can't come if you touch.'

There were more phone calls that night – buyers for the golf sticks and guitar, and another offer of weekend stable work. The bantams were laying, the potatoes were growing, and Shane pulled the first radishes, crisp and red and round, to share with Tom and Jed.

Then on Monday Shane brought home a letter which threw a big black shadow.

• Thirteen •
Camp

'It's about the class camp, Mum. It's going to be at a lake and there'll be swimming and walks in the bush.'

His mother didn't reply till she'd read the letter. Then all she said was, 'You can't go.'

'Can't go? Can't go! But everyone's going. Why can't I? It's not fair!'

'Because it costs fifty dollars. And we can't afford it.'

Fifty dollars. Seventeen trolleys. And it was only weeks away.

'Sorry, Shane,' his mother said. 'I know it's tough. But there'll be other camps. And please God, Dad won't always be on the dole.'

'But we've been doing work for this one for ages. All about aquatic life and snakes and . . . it's not fair,' he repeated, trailing off when he saw his mother's face. It was no use. Then he made one last try. 'But the dole's money, Mum. You said Dad got a cheque.'

'Not the sort of money we like taking, Shane. For people who've always earned their living and paid their own way . . . It's hard . . . '

He didn't come to tea when she called. She called again, 'Shane, your dinner's getting cold.' Then, 'Shane, stop sulking and come at once.'

He had slammed the door but he wasn't sulking. He was just blotted out. Blotted out with disappointment. And shame. He'd be the only kid not going. It was bad enough wearing hand-me-down jeans that he'd ripped the labels off, op shop sneakers and T-shirts, and never having money for the tuckshop. But he'd learnt to pretend he didn't care about any of that. Pretend to the other kids. Even to himself.

But not going on the camp. Everyone would know his parents couldn't afford the fee.

Dad knocked later. 'May I come in, Shane? We need to talk.'

Shane made a muffled sound that could have been 'No,' or could have been 'Yes'. Dad chose to think it was 'Yes'. He sat down on the bed beside Shane and put his arm around him. 'It's tough about the camp. I'm as disappointed as you. Not that we had that sort of thing when I was at school. But I know how you must feel.'

'Why can't we afford it, Dad? I'll earn more trolley money and I'll pay you back. We've sold the pavers and all, and you're starting to have mowing jobs. And you're fixing the trolleys.

And you're getting the dole now.'

His father gave a laugh that wasn't funny. 'The dole,' he said bitterly.

And Shane realised that his father felt about the dole the same way as he felt about the jeans.

'Trouble is, Shane, that'll hardly keep us in food, let alone pay the bills – electricity, water, rates, car insurance and registration, petrol, fares, clothes. And then there's the mortgage. If we don't keep up our payments, we'll lose the house.'

'Like Tom and Jed?'

Dad nodded.

'It's not fair,' Shane exclaimed.

'You're right. But that's how it is. We're using our savings for the mortgage each month, but they're not going to last forever.'

'How long?' Shane asked in a small voice.

'A couple more months.'

There wasn't anything else to say.

Then Shane offered, 'You can have all my trolley money, Dad. I didn't know about the bills.'

'No. And you shouldn't have to. I don't want you to worry about it. I just want you to understand if Mum and I sometimes do things that seem a bit hard.'

The class was buzzing with excitement when they handed in their camp forms. Shane shoved his mother's note into the pile. Then as they were going to recess, Miss Williams called him.

'You're not coming on the camp, Shane. I'm sorry. For family reasons your mother says. Is everything all right at home?'

Shane nodded without looking at her. But she persisted. 'Your mother's not sick, is she? Or is she having another baby?'

Shane shook his head. But the suggestion winded him.

Miss Williams didn't seem to notice. She smiled and said, 'Let me know if there's anything I can help with, won't you?'

Like fifty dollars, Shane thought, scuffing his way out to the playground.

'You not coming on the camp?'

'Can't your mum and dad afford it?'

'Your dad on the dole now?'

Shane couldn't bear the shame. 'I'm not coming because my grandpa's sick. And he's special.'

'But he doesn't live with you, does he?'

'So why have you got to stay home?'

'Is he dying?'

Another hit below the belt. Shane wished they'd all go off on the camp that instant and leave him alone.

Then he took out his trolley money. He'd show them. He said to a friend, 'Coming to the tuckshop?' and sauntered across the yard. He plunked down three dollars on the counter. 'A big bag of mixed lollies, please.' It felt good handing them round to everyone. It was a great way to stop their gobs. Trolley lollies, he grinned to himself. They'd be surprised if they knew how he got the money. That was his secret.

But there were eight days to go before the camp. And their comments niggled.

That night he asked his mother, 'You having another baby?'

'Who's been talking?'

'Nobody. I just wondered.'

'Yes, Shane. In May. Perhaps on your birthday.'

Shane felt winded again. *Another* baby! It was

probably the only present he'd get. 'I wonder if it will be a boy or a girl,' he said, trying not to sound as stunned as he felt.

She didn't look happy or excited either, just tired and sad. Shane patted her hand. 'That'll be great, Mum. I'll look forward to that,' he said, trying to sound pleased for her. 'Now I think I'll ring GP and tell him how the bantams are going.'

'Sorry, Shane. We had the phone cut off today.'

'But how can we sell things? And find out about Dad's jobs?'

'The fishing rod went today at last. So did the computer. There's not much else.'

Shane swallowed hard. There was still the car.

Next day Miss Williams said, 'Sorry to hear your grandpa's ill.' GP often featured in Shane's stories, so she felt she almost knew him.

Shane shuffled. 'Who told you?' Then changed the subject. 'Mum *is* having a baby. I asked last night.' At least that was the truth.

'That's something to look forward to,' she said.

But Shane didn't look happy or excited. He was overwhelmed by a sudden fear. Miss Williams had asked about his mother and she was pregnant. What if GP became ill, because he had said he was. What if his lie became horribly true? He had to find out if GP was all right. 'Please could I ring and see how GP is?'

'Now?'

Shane nodded, dumb with fear. If anything happened to GP . . .

'Come with me then. We'll see if you can use the office phone, just this once.' She recognised the panic, the urgency.

The receiver was heavy in his hand until GP's voice boomed out, 'Young rabbit! What's this all about? You brought me in from my tomatoes. Everything okay?'

'Yes, GP. The bantams are fine. And the radishes. Are you all right?'

'Nothing wrong with me. Fit as a fiddle. See you Saturday.'

Shane put down the receiver. Relief flooded

over him. Then shame again. Miss Williams was waiting across the room. GP's voice was so loud she would have heard every word. His stupid stupid lie . . . He wanted to bolt, but her hand was on his shoulder.

'Let's sit down and have a talk. I'm sure we can sort things out. Grandpa's all right now, so that's good. Is your dad unemployed?'

Shane nodded. 'But it's not his fault!' He was surprised to hear himself shouting. 'It's not his fault!'

'I'm sure it's not. And it makes all sorts of things very difficult. Like money for camp. I guess your parents feel they can't afford it.'

Shane nodded again miserably.

'But we've got a special fund for families having tough times in the recession. I'm sure we'll be able to help, so you won't miss out.'

• Fourteen •
Going Going . . .

Camp was great. Shane enjoyed the bush walks. And he got on well with his swimming. He was sorry when it was time to go home. Dad was waiting when the bus arrived at school. He shouldered Shane's swag. 'We're walking home.'

Shane thought nothing of it. There was so much to tell. But when they turned into the drive, the carport was empty. 'Is Mum out?' Shane asked, disappointed if he couldn't share all the stories of camp straightaway.

'No.'

'You've sold the car!'

'Yep. The old gas guzzler was due for registration. Got a pretty good price too.' Dad was trying to sound cheerful.

Shane felt hollow. What was left? The video camera? If they sold that, there would be no more photos of Shelley growing up, none at all of the new baby.

Over tea, baked beans again, Shane told of the

111

last three happy days. But underneath, the thought of the red Ford in another carport nagged.

Tom and Jed didn't even say, 'Told you so.' But they borrowed GP's mower and Dad's clippers to tidy up round their house on Saturday. The auction was on Tuesday.

Then Dad took them all fishing. They had a good catch and Mum invited them to tea. But their mother didn't come. 'She thinks her black eye still shows,' Jed said.

On Sunday Dad announced, 'Today we'll organise our Christmas tree.'

'But Christmas is still six weeks away.'

'It's not going to be an ordinary tree. It needs six weeks.'

Shane grinned. Dad was not an ordinary dad. 'Who wants an ordinary tree?'

Dad took the hatchet and they went to the creek. 'A bamboo tree?'

'You'll see,' Dad replied, chopping a thick stem. 'Have a go.'

Shane chose and chopped carefully. When they had two bundles, 'Enough,' Dad said, and they carried them home.

'What's going on?' Tom and Jed wanted to know.

'Give us a hand and you'll find out,' Dad invited. They stripped all the leaves. 'Mulch for the pumpkin patch.' Shoots were already going in all directions from the seeds they'd saved and planted.

'Now imagine you're building a little teepee.' They stuck the bamboos into the ground Dad had dug, making a tall cone. Then from his pocket he pulled a packet of bean seeds. 'Scarlet runners. By Christmas they'll be to the top and covered with red flowers. Pretty as any tree.'

Shane could see it already in his mind. He was proud and sad at the same time. Proud of Dad for thinking of a Christmas tree that wouldn't cost a cent, that would grow food. Sad realising that Tom and Jed wouldn't be there to see it. Christmas without Tom and Jed he couldn't imagine.

In the afternoon they went can-collecting, each knowing there wouldn't be many more such expeditions.

Tuesday was fine and warm. Dad had mowed their lawn and the nature strip all along. And he'd rebuilt the gatepost. Tom and Jed were staying home from school. But Shane's parents made him go.

He couldn't keep his mind on the work, though it was about what they'd done at camp. He couldn't even listen to the story Miss Williams was reading. He fidgeted and stared out the window and finally was in trouble. When she said, 'I think you'll have to finish your work after school,' he couldn't bear it any longer.

'Not today please,' he begged. 'Tom and Jed's house is being sold at two o'clock. I must find out what's happened.' He ran all the way. Panting and sweating, he saw SOLD slapped across the auction board.

'Going, going, gone,' Tom intoned.

'All done,' Jed said.

'We move out the week before Christmas,' said Tom.

'Just have to find somewhere to go,' said Jed.

They stared blankly at the sign.

'Come and see the bantams,' Shane invited.

The next night his parents had another row. They were washing up when Mum said, 'I've got a job.'

'A job?' Dad repeated. 'But I don't want you going out to work. You're pregnant. And what about Shelley?'

Mum said, 'It'll help with the mortgage.'

'Of course it would help. But we can manage, Jen, without you . . . Especially now with the baby coming.'

'If only we could,' Mum said. 'But you know . . . '

'I know I don't want my pregnant wife going out to work. What's the job anyway?'

'Cleaning toilets at the bus station in town.'

Dad dropped the plate he was wiping. It

smashed into five pieces. But his parents didn't even seem to notice. 'Cleaning toilets! My wife cleaning toilets!'

'I do it at home. Someone's got to do it. It's only a couple of hours a day, if that makes it any better, so you can look after Shelley. And there were over a hundred women after the job.'

'Did you tell them you were pregnant?'

Mum shook her head.

Dad stared down at the broken plate, then stepped on it deliberately, crushing each piece. 'So I'm mucking out stables for race horses and you're cleaning toilets to keep a roof over our heads.'

Shane went out to the bantams. 'Come on, Shelley. We'll see if the banties have laid any eggs for your brekkie.'

• Fifteen •
Gone . . . to a New Home

The day the holidays began, the taxi truck came to Tom and Jed's. It didn't take long to load the furniture. Some had already been sold.

'We'll give you a ring when we're dug in somewhere,' Tom said.

'Our phone's cut off.'

'But you've still got your dad,' Jed said.

Shane could hear the pain and the longing in his voice. 'We'll go fishing in the holidays,' he suggested and was glad to see the bleakness in their faces lighten for a moment. 'And here's something each.' He pressed two of his little cars into their hands.

Then they were gone. Gone. And they'd been there forever.

Shane went along to the church and sat in the rainbow quiet. Hurting as if his hands had been cut off. Tom and Jed.

After a while he noticed the lady beside him. Quiet, caring, knowing he was hurting. It helped

just having her there. He smiled his thanks, then found himself telling her everything. She listened, hands clasped. He felt better for sharing.

'Your mum must eat well for the baby,' she said, giving him an extra big bag of goodies. 'Come again before Christmas, won't you. I've missed you.'

Scouting for cans next day Shane ran into Troy, the boy who'd taken GP's orange. Troy's father had lost his job two months ago and at first he'd tried to hang around. Shane had felt sorry for him and suggested letting him join their gang. But Tom and Jed had told him not to be stupid. There was little enough return from the cans without sharing it. And they'd sent him packing.

Now here was Troy, on their beat. And Shane was alone. For a moment he was scared. He expected the old bully tactics. But Troy was chastened. 'Can we be partners?' he asked. Nobody could replace Tom and Jed. But Troy was big too. Other boys wouldn't take him on or move into his territory. Shane decided it was his safest move. At least it wouldn't be so lonely.

Can-collecting mornings, trolley-scouting afternoons, looking after Shelley while Mum worked, going with Dad, fishing, mowing, mucking out, to the supermarket and the Salvos – Shane was proud to add his bit to the housekeeping.

The Christmas tree had grown just as Dad had said. The scarlet runners had lived up to their name, spiralling higher up the bamboo teepee each day, reaching the very top in time for Christmas, leafy green hung with red flower clusters. Shane gave radishes to GP, his church friend, the op shop lady and the checkout girl. The Salvos gave a pudding and a cake, a toy for Shelley and a book for Shane. Thomasina, Jedda, Bimbi and Brown Beauty each gave an egg.

On Christmas Eve a card came from Tom and Jed with their new address and straightaway Shane wrote to them to fix their fishing day in the New Year.

But Christmas wasn't the same without Tom

and Jed, showing presents, sharing goes on bikes and skateboards. And the new neighbours kept to themselves. They didn't have children.

Beans began to set and Shane watched them grow. The potatoes flowered white and mauve, and the pumpkins flaunted great yellow blossom bowls which bees loved. Shane peered daily to see which were turning into pumpkins and announced the new tally at teatime.

So the holidays went by. Mum grew thinner and Shane watched the baby bulge beginning. Dad went to the employment office and the library, wrote lots of letters, went for some interviews in his best suit, but didn't get a job. He whistled a lot and did the housework. Shane wasn't sorry when school went back.

Two weeks into the term Shane was surprised to see GP's old car when he came home. GP was sitting in the kitchen with Mum and Dad, while Shelley played with saucepans.

Dad pulled out a chair for him. 'Glad you're home, Shane. It's a family conference. We can't keep up the mortgage payments much longer. And GP has invited us to live with him.'

Shane gulped. It had been looming closer so long and now the mortgage had come out of the shadows as the monster it sounded, a gigantic maw swallowing everything, swallowing the only home he had ever known. But Shelley banged lids happily. She was too young to understand.

121

Mum and Dad and GP were all watching him. 'Well, what do you think, Shane? It's very kind of GP, isn't it?' Mum said.

'Oh yes, GP, it's good of you.' GP was the best grandpa in the world. But GP's house was small. It was dark. And it smelled. 'But where would we all fit?'

'GP's giving us the front room, and we'll have Shelley in with us. You can sleep with GP. Or in the lounge.'

GP said, 'Not much fun sleeping with me. I snore. And your dad will be watching cricket on TV in the lounge. I reckon what we should do is make a sleep-out for Shane.'

A sleep-out. That sounded exciting. Fresh air. It wouldn't smell.

'We'll enclose the end of the back verandah. Like you had on the farm,' he said to Dad. 'And you'll be right on the spot to pick up more work. Plenty of stables. Who knows, you might land something regular.' He said to Mum, 'I can mind Shelley while you go to work. And be another pair of hands when the baby comes.'

It seemed to be all settled.

'The bantams?' Shane asked.

'They'll come too, of course.'

So would the beans, because they were already eating them. But the potatoes wouldn't be ready. Nor would the pumpkins. Bits were falling off the world.

It was too much to think about. Shane retreated to his refuge, the rainbow haven. His friend found him. They sat together without speaking. And gradually, in her company, Shane began to feel that everything would work out. Things would change. Like rainbows do. But in the end it would be all right. Different. But all right. He looked up at her. 'We're selling our house. The mortgage has won.'

'That's hard,' she said. 'Have you somewhere to go?'

'We're going to GP's. It'll be a squash. But he's going to build me a sleep-out.'

'That sounds fun,' she said. 'And you'll make lots of other friends at your new school.'

Shane nodded. 'But I'll miss you. And I don't mean for the goodies.'

'There'll be another place like this. There always is, if you search. It mightn't look the same. But it'll feel the same.'

Shane felt comforted as he carried home more powdered milk to help the baby's bones grow, more rolled oats to help Dad look for jobs, peanut butter and raisins for lunches.

Within days the sale sign was up on their house. And at the weekend he and Dad helped GP building the sleep-out. He helped Mum pack books, toys, clothes, and each time they went to GP's they took a load. He had to keep his room tidy, in case people came to

look at the house. That was an effort.

He and Troy still collected cans and he still spotted trolleys. The weeks slid by. Auction day came and he had to go to school. It was even worse than the day of Tom and Jed's auction.

Shane felt sick. Sick in his gut. How could he sit all day as if nothing was happening? He felt the money from his last trolley in his pocket, saw a bus coming and decided. He'd go to GP's. GP wouldn't tell.

GP was painting the sleep-out. He didn't seem surprised to see Shane. 'This is only undercoat. You're just in time to come with me and choose the real colour.'

They wandered in the hardware store examining all sorts of things. Shane chose yellow paint. 'It looks like sunshine.'

'Nice and bright,' GP agreed.

They painted together in companionable silence, Shane along the lower, GP the upper wall and ceiling. As they stood back admiring their work, GP said, 'Makes the rest of the place look a bit dingy. Have to see what we can do to brighten things up.'

Shane felt encouraged to say what was worrying him. 'There won't be any rainbows or light fairies for Shelley from Mum's vase when the blinds are down.'

'You're right. We must have rainbows. And I've got a surprise for you too.' He went to a cupboard and brought out a pair of vases, smaller than Mum's, but crystal also. He gave one to Shane and they took them to the kitchen to wash. 'They belonged to your dad's mother. I put them away after she died. I'm not big on dusting.'

They carried them back to the sitting room, dusted the mantelshelf and sat them at each end. 'Up with the blinds, young rabbit. And I'll open the windows.'

The afternoon sun flooded in with a little puff of breeze carrying garden scents. GP beamed as the long imprisoned rainbows burst across the walls and light fairies danced over the ceilings. 'Now that ought to make Shelley feel at home. And there's space here right in the middle for the big vase you gave your mum. We'll have to grow some flowers to pick. Cornflowers were always your gran's favourites. She loved blue. And I like snapdragons and marigolds. They're so cheerful. We'll choose next time we go shopping. Now I must get you home before your parents start worrying.'

Home. It wouldn't be home much longer. But with the blinds up and the windows open GP's was already feeling more like home. Shane could imagine the smell of fresh bread and pumpkin scones, rhubarb pie and orange cake wafting from GP's kitchen.

The man was pasting up the SOLD sign as GP chugged into the drive. Mum and Dad looked

126

sad but relieved. Shane thought of Tom, going, going, gone, and Jed, all done.

'Shane's been helping me to get the place ready today,' GP announced. 'We've got quite a bit to do yet, haven't we, young rabbit? But he can stay for a couple of days over Easter and we'll soon get it spruced up. It's great to have a helper. His sleep-out is looking so good I'm thinking of making one for myself at the other end of the verandah. Shelley and the baby can have the second bedroom then. We don't have to be sardines.'

Shane hugged GP. It would be good having him nearby at night.

His parents didn't say a word about him missing school and Mum wrote a note for the next day. Dad said, 'The house brought a fair price considering the recession, so we'll get something back. We haven't lost everything. I reckon the vegie garden helped. And people loved the bantams. Someone even wanted to buy them. But I said "No way." '

Shane squeezed Dad's hand. He hugged Mum and said, 'Do you think GP ought to take the vase now? We've made a safe place for it.'

'A good idea,' she agreed. They made a nest for it in a box of clothes and put it in the car.

Over Easter they built the bantam yard and brought Thomasina, Jedda, Bimbi and Brown Beauty across. And Shane spent the first night in his sleep-out. It was great to look out from his bed and see the stars.

On Easter morning he ran out to the bantams and found surprises in the nesting boxes. There were two eggs in glittering blue and pink foil, one for him and one for Shelley. And in one box there was a big rattly seed packet with a colourful picture. RAINBOW SWEETPEAS he read. In the other was a yellow netting bag bulging with shiny brown bulbs looking just like chocolate eggs. POT OF GOLD DAFFODILS the label said.

'Can we plant them today?' he asked GP.

'Sure can,' GP said. 'We'll watch them grow every day. And in the spring there'll be flowers for all the vases.'

In the afternoon GP organised an Easter egg hunt in the garden and invited the children from next door. They were Greek on one side and Indo-Chinese on the other.

Elena and Spyro said, 'You must come to us in a fortnight for our Easter. We always have a party under the vine arbour.'

'That's when we'll be moving in,' Shane said.

'A double celebration!' they said.

'Next year you'll have two New Years,' Anh and Pham said, 'because we celebrate Chinese New Year. And you can come to school with us. It's good to have friends on your first day.'

Elena and Spyro agreed. They all knew what it was to start afresh somewhere else.

Spyro said, 'Our dad might have a job for your dad. He needs someone reliable for the fish shop at nights and weekends.'

And Anh said, 'Our mum's been wondering if your mum might do some babysitting. She doesn't like leaving us on our own at night when she goes to the restaurant, especially now our new baby's come.'

Elena told him, 'Our cat's having kittens. Your grandpa said you can have one if you like.'

Shane knew now for sure that things would work out. Often different. Sometimes difficult. But all right in the end. Just as his friend at the rainbow church had said. He had Dad and Mum and Shelley and GP. Plus the baby coming. And new friends too. Right beside him.

Christobel Mattingley has been writing since
she was eight years old and had her first pieces
published in children's pages of magazines and
the newspaper. Her first book, *The Picnic Dog*,
was published in 1970, when she had three
young children. While they were growing up
she worked as a librarian in schools and in a
teachers' college. She has been self-employed
as a writer since 1974 and has travelled widely
in Australia and overseas, speaking in schools
and libraries.

She spent most of the 1980s working with
Aboriginal people, editing and researching the
epoch-making history *Survival in Our Own
Land*, which tells the story of the 150 years of
occupation of South Australia from the
Aboriginal point of view. In 1990 she was
awarded the Advance Australia Award for
service to literature.

The Sack is her thirty-first book for
children. Some have been translated, some
have been made into films for the ABC, some
have won awards in Australia and the United
States. Best of all, they have all made her
many friends.

THERE'S NUFFIN' LIKE A PUFFIN!
☆☆☆☆☆☆☆☆☆☆☆☆☆☆☆☆☆☆☆☆☆☆☆☆☆☆

No Gun for Asmir   Christobel Mattingley/Illustrated by
Elizabeth Honey

The gripping, true story of seven-year-old Asmir and his family, who
flee war-torn Sarajevo to seek asylum in Austria.

Emmaline Harris   Nette Hilton/Illustrated by John Burge

Emmaline Harris's father has just moved interstate with his new wife
and their new baby. And Emmaline's mum is going to marry Doug
Grenfell. So where does that leave Emmaline? Where does *she* belong?
Here is a moving, gently humorous story from this popular Australian
author.

Teacher's Secret   Michael Dugan/Illustrated by Jacqui Young

In the summer of 1920, Evie is about to start a new school year as the
only girl in the little Tintababbi school. But her new teacher is a
surprise and the secret in the schoolhouse garden changes Evie's life
for ever.

THERE'S NUFFIN' LIKE A PUFFIN!

☆☆☆☆☆☆☆☆☆☆☆☆☆☆☆☆☆☆☆☆☆☆☆☆☆☆☆☆☆

So Who Needs Lotto?   Libby Hathorn/Illustrated by Simon Kneebone

When Denise Albermarle arrives at Mimosa Primary School, she is such a show-off and a bully that everyone hates her. So when she begins to strike up a friendship with shy Cosmo Ravezzi, no one is more surprised than he is . . .

A Children's Book Council of Australia Notable Book, 1991.

The Lenski Kids and Dracula   Libby Hathorn/Illustrated by Peter Viska

The Lenski kids are the wildest, naughtiest kids in the neighbourhood – until Kim Kip arrives next door. She goes to acting school and is saving for a Harley Davidson motor bike, and is keen to do some babysitting . . .

The Twenty-Seventh Annual African Hippopotamus Race
Morris Lurie/Illustrated by Elizabeth Honey

Eight-year-old Edward trains very hard for this greatest of swimming marathons with no idea of the cunning and jealousy he'll meet from the other competitors. This best-selling story takes you behind the scenes and shows you just what it takes to become a champion.

Winner of the Young Australians' Best Book Award (YABBA) 1986.

THERE'S NUFFIN' LIKE A PUFFIN!

☆☆☆☆☆☆☆☆☆☆☆☆☆☆☆☆☆☆☆☆☆☆☆☆☆☆☆☆☆

Butterfingers   Margaret Clark/Illustrated by Bettina Guthridge

It isn't much fun being the clumsiest kid at Mango Street Primary School. Stacey 'Butterfingers' Martin sure has a problem, and it's a real hassle for everyone, especially Mandy. But after they go to the fun park for Mandy's birthday, something *very* weird happens. Or is the answer as simple as Mandy thinks it is?

Weird Warren   Margaret Clark/Illustrated by Bettina Guthridge

Weird Warren worries about *everything*. He drives all the kids in Year Six at Mango Street Primary School round the bend – in fact, he's a Major Problem. It's just not cool to worry as much as he does, and it's not making life any easier for his friend Fergus. But then comes the Eskimo project, which has Warren stuck in more ways than one, and Fergus is determined to find him a cure!

Against the Odds   Robin Klein/Illustrated by Bill Wood

Five improbable stories from a master storyteller. A nine-year-old girl rids a town of aliens, a genie brings more than magic to suburbia and a pocket-sized visitor gives the gift of confidence to a shy boy.

Shortlisted for the 1989 NSW Premier's Literary Awards.